California Girl Chronicles

Brea's Big Break

By Michelle Gamble-Risley

WWW.3LPUBLISHING.COM

Library of Congress Control Number: 2012934267

ISBN-13: 9780985266905

California Girl Chronicles: Brea's Big Break Softcover Edition 2012

Printed in the United States of America

For more information about special discounts for bulk purchases, please contact 3L Publishing at 916.300.8012 or log onto our website at www.3LPublishing.com.

Author photo by Gail Shoop-Lamy

Book design by Erin Pace-Molina

Cover image copyright Forewer/Shutterstock

To Sonja Fisher, my friend and supporter who makes me laugh and stay positive. You have embraced and helped move this project forward as if it were your own book. Love and appreciate you Sonja. You rock! And together we're going to make Brea famous!

Acknowledgments

Thank you to Russell Risley who has been so loving and supportive about helping me move this book series forward. You are my rock.

Thank you to Erin Pace-Molina. You have made Brea "sick and sexy-fied". You have also been such a great talent in everything I do and back me up at every turn. You can't buy that kind of loyalty.

Thank you to the rest of the 3L Publishing team for always being helpful and loyal. You know who you are!

Finally, thank you to the supernatural and ethereal Brea. You have become an imaginary muse. I love playing and "manipulating" your world!

Thank you to Alia Mendonsa whose temptation to read the second book resulted in an offer to proofread free of charge. Now that's called being hooked!

Prologue

My name is Brea Harper, and I am the quintessential California girl. I am blonde, fabulously tall, pretty and smart. I'm a screenwriter, but often get mistaken for an actress since I live in Los Angeles among the other pretty people. My desire to write screenplays has nothing to do with fame or glamour. I love to write. Period. It's how I express my creativity and fulfill my artistic impulses. I live in a small apartment near Hollywood with my best friend Denise, who as you might know already, is quite a live wire and loads of fun. Last I told you, she was having an affair with her boss at the software company where she works. They're still screwing all over the building, but they see other people. Another dear and new friend is Maya, my feisty and fierce Latina friend, who works for my former lover Kale.

Ah, Kale – now you are probably wondering what happened after I betrayed my blonde Adonis producer-boyfriend Kale with that loser Drew. Well, the night in question went like this. I never showed up. "What?" you cry in objection. Yes, I know you're all so disappointed in me and wonder how

I could have left it all messed up like that. I guess the truth is I didn't want to face the consequences. I had absolutely nothing I could have said in my own defense. Justifying betrayal is just as sick as the act of committing betrayal. I had fallen for Kale, down to my DNA and did not want to justify bad behavior or attempt to blame anyone but myself; therefore, no explanation existed to invalidate Kale's feelings.

Instead, I wrote him a simple letter of apology, stating that my karma was badly damaged, and I hoped he would forgive me. He didn't respond to my heartfelt letter. Instead, I received a phone call asking me to come to a meeting to discuss revisions on my script *California Girl Chronicles,* which Kale's production company had recently purchased.

This meeting is where our story begins.

Chapter 1

I arrived at the pristine offices where, as usual, Erin the receptionist, greeted me with a warm smile. Every time I saw Erin, I intended to ask her out to drinks. She was so sweet and charming. I knew she would make a great girlfriend. She offered the requisite Perrier and brought it out and placed it on a coaster in front of me. I was nervous. I had not seen Kale in weeks. He had been in Arizona on the set of his new movie. I missed him even though I had no right to miss him. I had thought about calling him several times, but realized he needed time and distance away from me. As I sipped my Perrier, Erin smiled at me.

"You look so pretty," she offered.

I looked down at my collared, white blouse and silver-colored skirt. I had dressed conservatively but sexy enough to remind Kale of what he was missing. I was a screenwriter now, after all, and I ought to dress the part. I had long since ditched my bikini shop dresses with the awful, suggestive slogans on the front.

"Thanks," I replied and shifted uncomfortably. "You know, Erin, we should go out for drinks sometime," I offered.

"You know, a girl's night out."

Erin smiled and replied, "Yeah, I would like that."

Then a handsome man with dark hair and sophisticated, squared-off glasses came to the doorway and waved at me. "Brea?" he asked.

I stood up, "Yes."

"Come on in," he said as he moved back into the office.

I got up and followed behind him. What I saw from behind was impressive, and I found myself staring.

He glanced over his shoulder with a broad smile. "My name is Curtis. I'm also one of your executive producers. I'm glad to meet you," he said with a grin and a wink.

The wink threw me. It was flirtatious, especially combined with that grin. This Curtis guy was super hot, too. I had to literally unglue my eyes off his sculpted backside. I didn't want him to catch me looking – not a good start to my new job. I imagined that Kale might not appreciate this attraction right now either. I walked into an empty conference room. Kale wasn't there yet and I sat across from Curtis, who couldn't suppress his smile.

Curtis was so obviously smitten it was almost embarrassing. I couldn't help it. I had to smile back. Our eyes locked for a moment, and then I felt Kale's energy enter the room first, followed by his physical body. My back was to him, but an electric surge went through my entire body and made me quit smiling. I shifted and looked. There he was: my blonde, handsome, tall, lean and muscular man. He looked so stunningly radiant, it was hard for me not to touch him or go to him. I shoved my hands under my butt and shifted hard on them.

Unfortunately, behind him followed a short, cute brunette. More female energy in the room calmed me down, but I wondered who she was. She looked fresh with silky, unblemished white skin, radiant and pretty in a natural way. She followed closely behind Kale, and I wondered immediately about their intimate distance, as she was in his personal space. He didn't seem to notice or mind, which raised my sensitivity to the potential that my lover had moved on. I felt like crying, but I quickly got my emotions under control.

Kale looked me straight in the eyes as he said, "Brea, this is Monica. She is the script supervisor. She will be working with you directly on script notes." As he said this, his blue-green eyes stayed fixed on mine. It felt intense, and I wanted to look away, but I committed to maintaining eye contact.

"Okay," I replied quietly as insecurity raged through me – not just because of my fear that he had moved on, but also because here was Monica and something about "script notes" and whatever that meant, good or bad. I figured I would find out soon enough. I looked shyly down and asked, "How was Arizona?"

"Good. Look, we have some notes for you," he said and shifted toward Monica, who handed me a script with different colored pages.

I glanced at the first set of colored pages, which were typed out notes regarding pieces of dialogue. I closed the script with the intention of examining it privately later and not falling apart in front of these people. "Okay, can I look at these in my office?"

"Speaking of," said Kale, "your new office is down the hall, last door on the left."

"Oh," I replied surprised. I hadn't realized they were going to give me an office.

"You can work from home or use the office; it's up to you," said Kale. "Now I have another meeting. Any questions?"

I shook my head. As Kale got up, our eyes locked in a searing gaze. Monica looked from me to Kale. She grabbed her briefcase to avert her eyes. She looked uncomfortable. I again had an impulse to grab him, kiss him and do him right on the conference table, which of course, was not going to happen. Then he lifted his gaze and walked out. I stood there like a starstruck child – that is, until I felt Curtis walk up behind me.

Curtis was taller and leaned over to whisper in my ear, "You shouldn't stare so hard."

"What?" I asked as I regained my senses.

"Girl like you, wasting your time staring at that guy? You should go out with me instead," he said with a quiet laugh.

"I don't think so," I replied as I turned and met his eyes. "Bad idea, don't you think?"

"Probably," he said and laughed again. "But undoubtedly worth it. Let me show you to your office."

He walked me up the hallway, opened the door to a cute corner office with big picture windows, and stepped aside so I could walk in. A big-screen iMac sat on the barren cherrywood desktop with a phone next to it. The office was devoid of personality. I would soon rectify that.

"We need your revisions by Friday," he said flatly. "A current copy of the script is on the network in the intranet file labeled "Calif. Girl." Just pull it over, and you're good. If need any help, ask Erin."

I walked in and sat down. Curtis followed and before I knew it, he had aggressively turned my chair to face him. "If you need anything else, call me. Extension 12," he said and winked in that sexy way again.

He was stunning and shocking all rolled up into this dark, sexy man. He had just made his intentions quite clear. I wasn't planning to enlist his "anything else" offer, but I filed it in my memory for future reference if I needed any kind of favor. I turned to look at my new view – the hazy outline of buildings and palm trees in the afternoon smog and the rolling Hollywood Hills in the foreground. I sighed and smiled. It felt like a real "I-made-it" moment.

Chapter 2

Later that week, I met Maya at a small café up the street from the office. It was a Coffee Bean & Tea Leaf with patio furniture sitting on the terrace outside of the main street. I was sitting in the cool morning sunshine, sipping my hazelnut-flavored coffee when a shadow passed over my table. I looked up to find Curtis standing there. I had not seen him much that week after our initial encounter, but every time I passed him in the hallway, he winked and grinned. He seemed like an affable, flirtatious guy, and he was really cute. Despite our mutual attraction, I had no desire to start up with him. I kept holding out hope for some kind of peace treaty with Kale, and I knew a liaison with his executive producer would err on the side of bad taste and ill-advised company behavior. Yet here he was, acting all cheerful and smiling.

"Hey, how's it going?" he asked with that familiar grin.

"Good," I replied, taking another sip of coffee.

He moved forward and asked, "Can I sit?"

I motioned for him to sit and he did. Maya would be here soon and deflect any overt come-ons, so I felt comfortable. "How long have you been working with Kale?" I asked.

"About five years," he replied.

"Really? That's pretty long for this town," I said.

"Nah, good relationships last," he replied and eyed me for a moment. "You know, Kale mentioned you two went out."

"Is that all he said?" I asked, feeling out the situation. I hoped Kale had not told him about the mess I had made because it was embarrassing.

"Pretty much," he said. "He's kind of private. Are you still seeing him?"

"No," I said and looked down.

"No?" he asked as he cocked his head to try and grab my attention again. "You're single?"

"Yes, but … "

"But?"

"But I'm not looking," I said with disinterest. I wanted some firm boundaries set with Curtis right away.

Curtis seemed entertained and laughed. "That so?"

And then Maya showed up and eyed Curtis with suspicion. I stood up and she kissed me on each cheek European style and said, "Hola, chica."

"Maya, this is my executive producer, Curtis," I said as I sat back down.

Maya nodded and took a seat between us at the small table. Curtis looked at Maya who seemed serious and guarded. He took it as a cue and stood up. He nodded at Maya and grinned at me, "Hey, nice to meet you. I have a meeting so I'll see you later," he said and waved as he left.

"Oh I see, yes, he'll see you later, will he?" she said with a look that suggested disapproval.

"Come on! I work for him," I protested at the suggestion.

"Sí, and it's best you keep thinking that way, chica," she replied.

"Oh, but they're going to cast the movie soon." I laughed. "That will be fun!"

"Kale said you never play with the talent." She looked at me seriously again.

"But I can look," I said with a laugh. Then I shifted and leaned forward to speak in a low voice. "Is Kale seeing someone new?"

Maya looked uncomfortable. "We should not speak of this," she warned.

"Oh, come on. I won't tell," I reassured her.

Maya looked ready to squeal when the person in question, Kale, walked up. I made a mental note not to take breakfast so close to the office. He looked at the two of us and smiled. My heart jumped in my chest, and I shifted away. I felt a surge of desire and frustration. I missed him. He looked me straight in the eyes and nodded. God, this man was striking to look at. His deep blue-green eyes always lit my fire. I also found his well-built body balanced by his broad, lightly hairy chest a big turn on. I feared I might need to wipe drool away.

"Ladies, you having a nice breakfast?" he asked, looking right at me.

"Sí," replied Maya. "You join us, yes?"

Kale shook his head and maintained my gaze. "No, meetings all morning, but you enjoy," he replied and walked on.

My stare stayed fixed on his sculpted backside – that made two perfectly shaped derrieres in one morning, and I was in heaven. He was wearing slacks and a white shirt and tie. He was a "suit," that was for sure, but one who looked more like a male model with those high, angular cheekbones and his perfectly slicked-back blonde hair. He didn't normally wear suits, so I figured something was up today – maybe with the financiers. He had once said he had to look the part when he met with the money people. He normally wore casual T-shirts and jeans – all, of course, expensive and pressed. He never looked sloppy.

"You feel for him?" asked Maya.

I nodded ever so slightly and felt my eyes water a little. I quickly composed myself and responded, "Yes, but I fucked it up."

Maya nodded, "Sí, and he a good guy."

Was she rubbing salt in my wound? I didn't think she meant to, but she wasn't making me feel any better. I sulked for a moment, then sighed and sucked in air. Maya changed the subject and mentioned she was going to Mexico for a couple of weeks to see family. I listened but was distracted. It hit me how hard it was going to be working by Kale's side in these coming months, but I was determined not to mess up my first professional screenwriting job. I didn't need to compound everything and make it worse.

My mind momentarily drifted to Drew, my love-hate nemesis. I had not seen him since the day he confessed his love and his desire to avoid any significant commitment that could lead to marriage. Remember, I had an affair with Drew, got caught, and broke Kale's heart. In turn, Drew confessed his relationship issues, and in turn broke my heart. We have not even texted or emailed. I needed to stay away from him. Our encounters had ruined everything with Kale – and here I was full of feelings of loss, longing and despair with no one to blame but my weak self.

Maya noticed the sadness in my eyes. "You need to move on, chica," she urged. "You can't let this go on. It makes you sad. I don't like you sad. You're too beautiful."

I sighed and nodded. "You have fun in Mexico. I'll miss you."

Maya stood up and leaned over to hug me. "Be safe," I said.

"Sí," she replied and stepped back. She smiled and left with a cheerful step and spring. She seemed happy. I realized I had not asked her a thing about her own life. I decided to find out what was putting that spring in her step when she came home.

A short time later, I walked into the office to find Curtis and Kale in a heated discussion with Monica. I walked right into it and all three turned and looked at me with unhappiness. I was stunned and wondered what it was all about. Monica stood there and stared at me. She seemed very hesitant and then finally shoved a stack of notes at me.

"What's this?"

Monica's eyes shifted from Kale to Curtis and then back to me. "Notes on your revisions."

"Oh, okay," I replied uncertainly. I started to read them.

My eyes widened. "This is a complete rewrite," I protested. "Am I not doing what you want?" I asked with insecurity coursing through my veins.

Kale looked at Curtis and then at me and sighed. "Just do the revisions," he replied in an unpleasant way. Kale turned and walked stridently back to his office. He looked annoyed and frustrated.

Curtis stared at me. "Well, you heard him," he said.

Monica shrugged and walked away toward Kale's office, which bothered me. She had his ear, and she was the script supervisor, not the writer. Something about that on both a personal and professional level bothered me. I wasn't sure what the subtext in that interaction meant. Anxiety rushed through my mind. I wasn't feeling like myself at all – it was all much too serious. I needed comic relief – all good California girls can joke their way through any situation. I tried to think of something entertaining to say.

"This isn't *Waterworld,*" I said with a sniff.

Curtis grinned at me. He got the joke and replied, "You better hope not." He moved in closer, and I looked up from the notes. He smiled at me in a genuine way. "You want some unsolicited advice?"

I nodded, and he stared at me for one more second. "You should just sleep with me and get it over with."

He laughed and snickered. I think my mouth must have dropped open. He wasn't being the least bit threatening. Was this sexual harassment? What did he mean by that? And what did any of it have to do with the script notes? He touched my shoulder and rubbed it, and then he turned and walked away. I felt like a confused child. Between the artistic insecurity and the puzzling comment, I was just lost. I decided to go back to my office and follow the script notes to the letter.

Chapter 3

That night, I went home tired. Denise wasn't home, as was mostly the case these days. She and her boss spent most nights together, leaving the apartment partially paid for by her but virtually vacant. She kept some of her clothes here still, but it was all for appearances. She had set up camp at her boss' home in Calabasas. I was fine with it. I was working late and fully consumed in my professional life. I didn't want any distractions, and Denise was – if anything else – good for distractions. She was either getting dressed to leave or talking about her latest work drama that was heightened by the affair with her boss. I mostly listened and laughed at the dramatic subterfuge she managed to conjure up.

I was eating some leftover lasagna when a knock came to my door. I wasn't expecting anyone, so I was surprised to find Letty standing there when I opened the door. She had dyed her hair purple and was wearing chic white sunglasses that were a throwback to '80 retro Raybans.

"Letty!" I cried as she sprung on me so that we fell backward into my apartment onto the sage green carpet.

She laughed uproariously and straddled me as I fell onto

my back. She pretended to slap me for a moment and then got up. "Doll face!" she cried with enthusiasm. "Let's get out of here! You look bored."

I started laughing. She wasn't my boss anymore, as I had said good-bye to what Kale had called "bikini hell" a little over two months ago. Letty, in true style and form, wore a jean mini-skirt with a pink T-shirt that said "Up Yours!" which clashed with her purple hair. She looked appropriately chic and rebellious all at once.

I agreed to go to the local dive bar and hang out. I pulled on a simple pair of jeans, platform sandals and my own familiar T-shirt with my least favorite but still sentimental phrase on it: "Love My Coconuts." I wore it to honor Letty, who I had not seen in months.

About 30 minutes later, we found ourselves sitting on barstools, eating stale tiny pretzels and drinking shots of Patron. I had two shots and that was quite enough to catch a zing of a buzz. Letty had three shots, and she was drunk and happy. She giggled her way through the conversation, which eventually led to questions about Drew's fate. She said he quit the day after I left.

"Whore!" she crowed. "He left me! It's all your fault." She laughed. She threw a pretzel and hit my forehead.

I began laughing. "Sorry! But you didn't lose much," I replied and threw a pretzel back.

"Oh, fuck him," she cried. "You know he told me he fucked you ... twice!" she started cackling.

In the past, this announcement would have made me angry.

Now, I was just disgusted and not surprised. "I see, he kissed and told," I replied.

Letty leaned in with a grin. "I fucked him once in the back room," she admitted and laughed. "It was okay," she added.

"Supply closets," I muttered in disgust. "Well, he fucked many," I said as I lifted my glass. "Cheers!"

Letty obliged back, and our glasses made a "clink" as they purposefully collided. Letty settled down a moment and became thoughtful. "I think he really loved you, Brea."

I glanced over at her and considered that suggestion. "Maybe," I replied. "He hurt me though, and that's enough of that."

"Hey, I got a part in a skincare commercial," she announced with pride. "It's national with lines," she added.

I nodded. "That's really great! Good for you."

Later that evening, Letty and I parted ways. We made no future plans to see each other, but somehow I suspected it wouldn't be long. She mentioned that she was considering a job at the San Diego store and might move, but then she was flighty so I wasn't sure if she was serious. She seemed to be tinkering with the idea. She said her on-again, off-again boyfriend Rocco had moved, but that she wasn't sure she should follow. Since I was in no position to preach about moving for boyfriends, I refrained from giving her any advice.

I returned to the apartment to find the door ajar. I grabbed my cell phone to call 911 and peered in the door to see if anyone was there or something was disturbed. Upon a quick inspection everything appeared fine. I nervously crept and looked first in the two bedrooms that were directly across from each other and then the bathroom. No one was there. I began to wonder if I had left the door open on accident when I turned and was stunned to see Curtis standing in the doorway. My heart jumped up, and I grabbed and yanked the door fully open. It was nearly 9:00 p.m.

"Curtis!" I yelled. "What are you doing here?"

Curtis stepped forward and looked around. "You all right?"

"Jesus! Fine! What do you need?" I snapped at him.

Curtis extended another folder loaded with papers. My eyes nearly popped out of my head – more notes! "Kale asked me to drop these off so you could look them over before our production meeting in the morning."

I grabbed the stack and barked, "Since when are you a messenger?"

"I'm not," he stepped completely in and smiled at me. "I wanted to see you."

"Does Kale know that?" I sniped.

"No," he replied and then, made another move toward me. "Do you want to go for drinks?"

"No, I just came back," I replied and softened a bit as I realized I was yelling at one of my bosses, who for all intents and purposes really hadn't done anything to deserve the barking. After all, he didn't break into my apartment. And for all I knew, I had left that door ajar.

"Look, I'm harmless," he suddenly offered. "I just like you. Let's go out and relax. I'll tell you what's going on."

I stood upright and straight and mulled it over. I did want to know what was going on. Why was I getting almost a complete rewrite of the script? Should I be worried? Curtis seemed to be offering me somewhat of an olive branch. Then I became concerned about his obvious pursuit and the ramifications, so I quickly shook my head.

"No, really, I'm tired," I said. "Is that okay with you?"

Curtis nodded. "I get it."

He stepped into the hallway, turned and said, "See you tomorrow."

My heart was still racing. I wondered what was going on. I looked at the new stack of notes and sighed. I read a few and realized some of them conflicted with the last batch. Who was I supposed to follow? Too many chefs in the kitchen would make my job harder. I quickly decided to sit down with Kale in the morning and feel out the situation. I was all too aware that I was new at this, and I heard the stories about endless rewrites and scripts sitting with renewed options that never ended and studios never produced the films. I also feared they would shut down the entire project or replace me if I couldn't cut it. I was so consumed with worry that I didn't sleep well that night.

Chapter 4

I rose bright and early, grabbed some coffee from the pot and headed out the door with the goal of getting Kale alone before anyone came to the office. He worked out very early in his private gym at the office, so I planned to catch him then. I soon found myself walking straight down the hall to the gym connected to his office. I swung open the door and there was my insanely attractive man without a shirt on, working on the weights that build the upper back muscles. He was sweaty and glistened in the light. His eyes grew large when I walked in. The attraction was electric. I walked around the rowing machine straight toward him and stopped dead. No greetings were uttered, just silence. For a moment, we stared at each other. He released the weights, grabbed the white towel from around his neck and wiped his moist forehead and face.

"Brea?" He looked at me and waited.

"How are you?" I asked.

He stood there with a strangely intense look on his face. I stepped toward him, and he stepped back. Electricity pulsated between us. I moved forward again, and he moved back again. We then stood in a sort of Western stand off, each of us ready to draw our emotional weapons.

"Good," he finally answered, his deep blue-green eyes fixed on mine.

In a rare bold mood, I turned and shut the door I had walked through to give us privacy. I turned back around to find Kale's eyes fixed on my body. Again, silence fell between us. The desire was a fierce urge on both sides as the stares continued.

"Why'd you do that?" he asked in a way that almost dared me to make a move.

"I want to know if you miss me."

Eyes fixed on mine, he flatly replied, "Every day." He just stared at me with his intense, focused eyes.

I shifted in shock at the admission and asked, "You do?"

I moved toward him very slowly, waiting to see signs to stop. I soon found myself within inches of his body. He was aroused – and he wasn't doing anything to rebuff my advances. I slowly but steadily rose up on my tiptoes to reach his tulip-shaped mouth. Our lips brushed at first ever so gently and then Kale grabbed me by the waist in one swift action and pulled me upward so we were pressed together. We kissed so passionately. I had never kissed anyone so deeply and for so long. We kept kissing, and then Kale nudged me away with the same quickness.

"What do you want?" He turned away and grabbed his shirt.

I touched my now empty lips completely perplexed.

What did that mean? Was he ready to forgive me or not? "I — I don't understand."

"What?" he asked in a vacant way.

"The — the script notes," I stumbled. "Why so many? Are you going to fire me?"

Kale, who now wore a white racer-back tank top, softened his expression. He looked at me with those magnificent eyes. "No, the financiers wanted changes," he said quietly as he kept his gaze fixed on mine. "It's normal, sweetheart. Don't worry."

He had used his "sweetheart" endearment with me. I felt a surge of hope. I worked up my courage and walked back toward him. We kept our eyes on each other. He allowed me very close again. I reached up and stroked his rough cheek and then whispered in his ear, "Forgive me."

Kale grabbed me by each wrist and gently, but firmly pulled me forward. He made sure we were inches away from each other. I could feel his warm breath, eclipsed in desire – the same desire I felt just moments ago. We continued to stare at each other, and then Kale gently pushed me away so we were no longer touching. He looked down. I wasn't sure if he felt sad, mad or just beaten somehow. I felt an uncontrollable urge to cry, and the tears crept up and spilled over my lids onto my cheeks – this just set Kale off.

"Now you're going to cry?" he asked in a firm, even voice. He looked away, grabbed a water bottle and took a swig.

I wiped away the tears. "No," I replied.

Kale took another swig and said, "But you are." He

turned so I could not see his face. "Please don't cry," he softly pleaded.

I wiped away my tears and sighed. I decided to steel myself up and get a hold of my reeling emotions. I turned and opened the door. Just as it swung open I saw Monica about to walk in. Our eyes met. She looked startled by the look on my face.

"I'll have the changes to you by noon," I said and rushed away.

I could see her walk in the door to Kale and shut it behind her. I imagined her dropping the files she held and rushing into his arms. I had a terrible vision of them fucking right there on the weight seat. I quickly vanquished that terrible thought, but still the expression on her face was revealing. She was surprised and worried at the same time. It was at that moment that I suspected they had become lovers. Kale couldn't forgive me.

I returned to my office and plunged into the rewrites, determined to drown my pain in my work. Later, I headed out for lunch. I raced right out into the main building, jumped on the elevator, and smacked into a dark-haired, chisel-cheeked guy who was just getting off of the elevator. He was about 6 feet 1 inch and very well-built with broad, muscular shoulders. We hit each other straight on, and I fell backward right into the wall. He immediately grabbed me to help.

"Oh — sorry, darling," he said sweetly and politely.

I stood up and smiled brightly at him. "It's okay."

His eyebrow arched a little, and he fixed his gaze right

on me. "Damn, girl, you're fine," he said in such an earnest way. "You here for the auditions, too?"

"No, I don't act," I replied.

"Maybe you should," he grinned. "My name's Johnny."

"Brea," I replied, and I shook his outstretched hand and an electrical charge went straight between us. "What's the audition?" I asked.

"For some movie, *California Girl* something," he said.

"Oh, that's my movie. I wrote it. What part?"

"Drew something or other," he replied.

I found myself chuckling. He was a good fit. "You'd make a great Drew," I replied. "Good luck."

Johnny stared at me for a moment, nodded and went on his way. Man, this project was loaded with nothing but temptation. I pressed the elevator button and left.

Later that night, my old friend Lance invited me to drinks at the Roosevelt Hotel. I hadn't seen Lance in weeks, and our relationship had mellowed to the occasional text message. I wondered if he had started seeing someone new, but realized it wasn't my concern. I had no designs on him, and I wanted his attachment to me to fade. It seemed like it had, which is why I had agreed to drinks. When I arrived at the bar, I spotted him out on the terrace on one of the wicker loveseats with solid pewter-colored cushions. He waved at me and motioned to come out.

As I approached, I noticed he was mildly sweaty in a sexy kind of way and looked bright and happy to see me, but a little tired. He stood up and his green eyes sparkled as he leaned over in all of his tall glory and hugged me long and close. Since I was unattached, I didn't care. I let him press against me, and he became aroused. All greetings aside, we sat quietly down very close to each other. He told me he had been promoted to managing supervisor at the electrical plant. He started talking about hydraulics until I'm sure my eyes glazed over in boredom. The waitress brought out a bottle of Merlot for us to share, and he obliged and poured me a glass. We then did the requisite cheers and both sat back.

"How's the script coming?" he suddenly asked.

"Hard," I replied. "Lots of rewrites. Maybe I'm not cut out for this," I admitted.

"Giving up so soon?" he asked with a look of concern.

"No, just tired. Speaking of ... you look a little tired too," I said.

Lance contemplated the glass for a moment. "I got diagnosed with lymphoma," he said quietly.

"What?" I yelped with concern.

"Yep, not the bad kind, but I don't think there is a 'good' kind," he said. "Man, I don't know what's worse: the fucking disease or the doctor's appointments."

It occurred to me that he wasn't seeing someone else – he was preoccupied with doctor's appointments. I sat back in shock and asked, "You okay?"

He said he was okay, but that the treatment was rough. They were doing a course of radiation for now, which had just started. I listened and all of a sudden I burst into tears.

I'm not sure if it was the combination of Kale's rejection and the bad news or if I just needed to cry. I felt terrible crying in front of my sick friend. Lance frowned at me and suddenly pulled me very close. We hugged for the longest time. I sat back, and he leaned over and deeply kissed me. I didn't know how to feel about this. I allowed the kissing to continue, and then we both sat back and each took some sips of wine. I felt a strange sort of peacefulness.

"If I were to go tomorrow, I think I would be all right," said Lance, breaking the silence. "I've done what I wanted. Isn't that the most important thing? I mean, I'm not finished by any means, but you know, it's cool."

I was startled by this admission. I reflected briefly on my own short life. I didn't think I could be that practical. I had not yet done what I wanted. I wasn't even sure if I felt happy or not. I know in that moment with Lance, I felt glad to be there with him. I felt blessed to give him a brief moment of escape from his illness.

Then I leaned in very close to him and whispered, "Take me to your house."

Lance grinned and nodded at me. He tossed money on the table, and we headed for his new car, a white Toyota Camry. We didn't talk on the ride back. I held his hand in support and occasionally broke the grip and ran my fingertips up his arm. Before we even got out of the car, he was completely turned on. We walked arm-in-arm upstairs to his apartment where he used his key to open the door. He then gently swung me around and pushed me inward as he kissed me. As we breached the entrance, he kicked the door closed with the heel of his blue-and-black Sketcher and allowed his hands to move down my back and then forward to run across my breasts. I sucked in air totally caught off guard by his caress. It had been a while since I had been with anyone. I melted a bit and relaxed. I was letting off more than just sexual tension. The stress of the day was slowly rising off my shoulders, relieved by the alcohol that moved through my system.

Lance stood straight up and our eyes met. He took my blue blouse and swiftly and effectively unbuttoned it down the front. He then undid my bra and allowed it to drop to the floor. He reached for the ends of his own shirt, pulled it up and over his head and threw it to the floor. He then undid his pants and dropped them to reveal he had gone commando. His cock stood erect. I dropped to my knees and began to suck on him. My mouth moved forward and backward, and he moaned. He gently touched the top of my head.

"Yeah," he cried in a very un-Lance-like manner.

I was surprised by my typically nonverbal lover and decided to please him to the end. I figured a sick guy gets to have his way. After all, what if he got sicker and couldn't partake in sexual activities for a while? I thought I would make this one to remember so I sucked harder, determined for this to be his best blow job ever. He moaned as I ran my tongue up and down his shaft, and then plunged my mouth fully back over him. He was rock hard, and I was certain he might cum when he grabbed me and pulled me up.

He yanked me into his arms and carried me quickly to bed where he gently laid me back. My legs hung forward off of the bed, and he used his own leg to ease them apart so he could penetrate me. He slowly lowered his weight onto my body, and, as he entered, he let go of a deep moan that sounded more like relief. He leaned into me, kissed and sucked on my breast hard and fast. I was gripped in tension and lust. He began to fuck me with more vigor, then leaned forward and kissed me passionately on the lips. He was rhythmically fucking me with passionate intensity, and I reached around and grabbed his firm ass. My arousal went way up. He had a great, firm ass. I pushed him into me and began to rub on him. The tension built, and it felt so great. He moaned a little, and I knew he was about to cum, which turned me on even more. I gasped, and he moaned. We came together, and he grunted as I screamed. Then we both fell away from each other, breathing heavily.

I sat up on my elbows and brightly smiled at him. "If I were the last girl you fucked, would it be worth it?"

Lance let out a great laugh and replied, "Absolutely!"

He grabbed me and pulled me into a kiss. He then looked me straight in the eyes and said, "Thank you."

I nodded and said, "You're welcome ... stud!" and reached around and slapped his ass. We both laughed at that joke.

Chapter 5

Kale soon returned to Arizona for more on-set work. Other staffers from the office went with him so the place was quiet. I didn't mind. I was able to get a lot of work done, and believe me, the pile of notes for rewrites had only grown. I'd heard, though, that they were actively casting the movie and that Johnny, the hot man I'd met in the hallway, had won the Drew part. As I rewrote Drew's scenes, I wondered if he would see the movie. It occurred to me as I wrote the female lead that her words might make him feel the least bit repentant, but somehow I doubted it since Drew never expressed remorse. I was staring out my office window thinking about this when I heard a voice come from behind me.

"Are you busy?"

I turned around to find Monica standing in the doorway, which surprised me since she had gone with Kale to Arizona and was obviously back early. Monica had a strange energy about her. She was serious and quiet, and Kale didn't strike me as the type of guy who would go for the quiet, shy type. But I still didn't quite have a pulse on their relationship. He seemed distant with her in some settings and rarely looked at her with much interest, but occasionally they put off a lovers' vibe, especially since she always stood so close to him. I had only assumed they were together without confirmation. What did I have to say about it anyway? Kale was no longer my man.

"Sort of," I replied. "What's up?"

Monica walked in, set down a revised script and smiled. "Kale wants you to know he feels this is the shooting version."

"Am I done?" I asked.

A quizzical look passed over Monica's face as she replied, "Well — yeah, but you will be doing the on-set rewrites and new pages. You know, for when actors adlib."

I nodded and stared at her. She looked uncomfortable and shifted back toward the door. "Is it true?" she blurted.

I frowned and asked, "What?"

"That you were with Kale?" she asked and looked down toward the ground.

I felt indignant. I didn't feel comfortable around Kale's presumed lover, and her question was much too personal. I turned my chair back toward the window and skyline, searching for an answer to shut her down and not pique her curiosity. "I don't think we should be talking about Kale," I replied in a flat, unyielding tone.

Just then I heard a rustle and turned my chair back in time to see Monica's backside hustle out of the room and in her place, I rested my eyes on hot man-candy Johnny. He looked relaxed and had a big, open smile on his face.

"I remember you," I said brightly. "Heard you got the part of Drew. Good for you!" I chirped, admiring this gorgeous, dark-haired man with perfectly muscular arms.

"Can you grab a bite with me?" he asked. "I want to pick your brain."

I sat up and looked around my desk. I had nothing pressing, so I stood up and with enthusiasm replied, "Sure! Let's go."

Johnny stood in the doorway and waited for me. He allowed me to exit first like a gentleman. We made the requisite small talk as we walked to a Chinese café called Hop Singh up the street from the office. We sat on the back patio to eat noodles and chat. Johnny told me he started acting when he was 22, and he mentioned with a smirk how he got his first manager. The smirk piqued my curiosity.

"What's that about?" I asked and pointed at his grin.

"What?"

"That!" I countered and motioned again toward his expression.

He leaned in and started to explain. "Well, she pretty much signed me for sex," he admitted and chuckled with delight over it.

"What?" I frowned.

"Oh yeah, she was like a cougar, too," he said, "and she got me some great spots. I just had to fuck her twice a week."

I was taken aback and pulled away from him. "Really?" I asked with a frown.

He took a chopstick and shoved a noodle in his mouth as he said, "Really! But you know it's fucking Hollywood man. That shit happens all the time. Swing a dick, and there you go."

"No, I thought, you know, unions," I whispered.

Johnny waved off the suggestion. "Fuck that man. Chicks are as bad as guys. Look at me now, though."

I looked at him all right and frowned. "You don't feel ... dirty?"

Johnny waved off the suggestion, "Hell no! It's the biz and, fuck yeah, I've had fun, too!"

I leaned over and shoved another noodle in my mouth, pondering his amoral take on the whole thing. He didn't seem the least bit bothered by it. In fact, I got the impression he accepted and liked it.

"And you think you're going to get somewhere with me like that?" I flatly asked.

Johnny quit eating and looked me right in the eyes. "Fuck no!" he retorted. "You're hot and nice. I like you. And I like that you have real body parts." He chuckled as he looked down to take another bite.

I looked down at my body parts and nodded. "Yep! Real! No woman would purposefully make her boobs this small," I said with a laugh.

As Johnny talked about the business and his encounters on various movie sets, I started to like him. He was candid and enthusiastic about acting and his craft. He mentioned his last girlfriend was a major film star, but he wouldn't divulge her name. He did say he met her when he played a small role in one of her films. He said she was down-to-earth but had this strange obsession with her hair. She wanted to become famous for her hair like Jennifer Aniston. He thought it was a crazy goal, and he said her hair was okay, but that it wasn't likely going to create a national sensation.

"Why'd you break up?" I asked.

"I cut her hair off," he said, totally kidding and laughing with a gregarious outburst. "No, she went to film in Italy and met an Italian Antonio-Banderas-like guy. Dumped my white ass," he admitted with a smile that seemed out of place given his confession.

"And that makes you smile, why?"

"Come on, if she's so shallow ... fuck that shit! No big deal," he said as he shoved yet another noodle in his mouth and waved off the comment.

We soon finished lunch, and he walked me back to the office, continuing the upbeat chatter about meaningless parts he had played. He did admit that he thought the part of Drew was cool, but then he frowned at me. "The guy's a fucker, though."

Now he got it. I started laughing and realized I really liked him. "Yep," I replied and nodded, looking up into his soulful, light-grey eyes. "Hey, that was fun."

Johnny nodded and smiled with that same brightness. He then reached out and grabbed me by the arm, pulling me toward him. It occurred to me that getting involved with an actor wasn't such a good idea, so I pulled back a bit to resist.

He looked down at my arm and stepped forward instead. He leaned over and whispered, "Don't worry."

I looked up and met his gaze. He kissed my cheek. "I don't bite," he said as he inhaled my body lotion that was a mix of coconut and white ginger. "You smell amazing," he said as he sucked in air and closed his eyes with a peaceful smile.

I pulled back just a bit and smiled at him. I tentatively moved forward and ever so softly kissed his pink, soft lips. It was light and tender. Johnny opened his eyes and pulled back slightly. He lit up with the biggest smile and said, "I'm going to love this job."

Then he grinned, bowed as if he was a Japanese businessman and tipped his hand toward me. "You stay well, Miss Harper," he said in the most old-fashioned way, and he headed off toward the elevator.

I was utterly breathless as I watched his body disappear into the elevator. I stood outside the office door for at least a minute when the door pulled open, and there stood Monica startled by my appearance. She made a strange noise, stared at me, followed my eyes and watched the elevator doors close on Johnny. She gave me the strangest look and didn't say a word. She just left. I was puzzled – she was odd.

Chapter 6

The next day, Johnny texted me and asked me if I wanted to go rock climbing with him and stay overnight at his friend's cabin. Rock climbing? I wasn't into rock climbing, but I texted him back and said I would come and try my best. If anything, it sounded like a good challenge. We made plans for him to pick me up on Saturday morning at 8:00 a.m. because we were going north out of town toward Big Bear to a place called Castle Rock trailhead where we would hike to the southeast face to climb.

Johnny pulled up in a Chevy Blazer and literally honked from the parking lot of my apartment building. I peered out the window. Okay, he was a younger guy and the whole horn honk was just the sort of predictable thing he would do. I was wearing cute, light-blue North Face shorts, a plain, white tank top, and Converse tennis shoes. I wasn't completely illiterate about what to hike in and what to bring. I had promised Johnny I would bring a cooler with water and food for lunch, so I grabbed my blue-and-white cooler and raced out the door. I was up much too early for Denise, who had come in around 4:00 a.m. after a night of partying with her hunky boss.

When I got downstairs, I noticed another guy sitting in the front seat with Johnny. This guy, who immediately jumped out to help me, smiled and said his name was Ryan. Ryan was tall, lanky and overly cute with his sandy blonde hair cropped short to his head. His smile and his blue eyes were bright and warm.. He introduced himself, grabbed the cooler and allowed me to sit in the front seat. As I slid in, I realized two impossibly good-looking men, both of whom looked like they belonged on the cover of *GQ*, would be my companions for the day – and this realization made me smile with pleasure.

We drove the two hours to Big Bear and didn't talk about anything important. Johnny and Ryan mostly bantered back and forth, and I soon discovered they were roommates. Ryan, who admitted to being born with a silver spoon "up his ass," said his father was a big studio titan. He laughed that daddy paid his bills, which gave him loads of free time to rock climb, skydive, play soccer in three leagues and generally loaf around. When I asked if his daddy had any expectations for his future, he grinned and said, "No."

I don't think I've heard of a parent with fewer expectations than Ryan's "old man," as he occasionally referred to him. And the more he talked, his dad sounded like an interesting character. Ryan said his dad was an old-school surfer dude turned into a flip-flop-wearing executive who produced a string of blockbusters and landed at the top of the food chain. I filed away the thought that contact with Ryan might someday come in handy. Ryan also had the most playful eyes, and he talked to me with a huge smile that sparkled with mischief. I asked if he had a girlfriend to which he admitted he had five. I started laughing and asked how hard that was to juggle.

"Not hard at all," he said and tossed up his digital personal assistant, which I artfully caught between my hands.

I looked down at the planner and saw that he actually scheduled dates in rotation. I started laughing and threw it back at him. "Are you serious?"

"Absolutely," he replied with a laugh.

"I noticed Saturday night isn't scheduled," I said.

"Got to schedule time to meet new 'booty,'" he replied.

"Do you consider yourself a womanizer?" I asked as if I were interviewing him.

Ryan gave me such a delightful grin and said, "No, I just love women."

Johnny started laughing at that one, and they bumped knuckles in approval. I sat back and watched this scene. What should I read into this mutual admiration? I looked at Johnny now, slightly concerned about any trysts I might have with him. And he was one of the actors in the movie. Johnny must have sensed my apprehension because he briefly took his eyes off the road to wink at me. He then reached across the seat and gently rested his hand on my leg. I looked down and smiled. He was, if nothing else, a fun guy.

We arrived at the trailhead and unloaded. I jumped out

of the Blazer and took in the fresh pine scent. It felt really great to be out of the city and smog. Johnny and Ryan unloaded the gear and started prepping their equipment and ropes for the climb. We soon began our hike and ascended routes with names like Taj, The Murder Hole, Timeline and Crocs in the Moat. Ryan and Johnny managed to talk me into trying the less difficult climbs up the granite face.

I roped up with Johnny to climb as far as I could make it. He was understanding and didn't push me beyond what I felt comfortable. With more than innocent interest, I watched both men's arm and leg muscles flex as they pulled their way up the rocks. I was overtaken by lust, but managed to keep my cool. They were such good-looking guys – all muscular, sweaty and shimmering. It was a moment when I could have grabbed some popcorn and just entertained myself with a simple view of their bodies.

At one point, we stopped on a ledge where we could look down on the expanse of Big Bear Lake's west end – it was stunning. The water was a deep blue and the wind blew through the pine trees making a soft hum. Ryan joined us on the ledge, and we all sat down for a lunch of ham-and-cheese sandwiches and water. A peaceful calm settled between us as we gazed over the azure lake and the mountains covered in green pine trees with jagged peaks blanketed in white snowcaps.

Ryan unexpectedly reached across and patted my knee. He let his hand rest there a bit, and I felt strange and uncomfortable. Was he coming onto me? Johnny didn't notice or care if he did. When he flirted, he looked me right in the eyes and winked. I will admit that sitting on that ledge that afternoon with two incredibly sexy men was memorable. We didn't talk. We just enjoyed the view, smells and beauty. We were all hot, sweaty and pleasantly relaxed together as we did little else than eat sandwiches. It was perfect.

When we returned to the trailhead, we quietly loaded up the Blazer. Ryan said his family cabin was about 30 minutes from there. We left and drove through the windy roads at lake level. As we pulled up to the community of lakeside estates, I realized the word "cabin" probably didn't describe the "old man's pad," as Ryan described it. We pulled up to a wooded area with a gate. Ryan reached in his backpack and hit a button, which I assumed controlled the gate because it gently opened outward. Johnny pulled forward, and we drove another quarter of a mile along a narrow lane lined by pine trees before reaching the opening where a three-story cobblestone house trimmed in logs and knotty pine stood. Like I had with Kale's house, I kept my astonishment under wraps.

We piled out of the car, and Ryan walked ahead of us to open the front doors. He pushed them open to reveal a foray that lead straight into an enormous living room, which included a big glass wall looking out over the lake. The home was decorated with rustic furniture and brown leather sofas and chairs. Nappy sage-colored throw blankets were tossed over the tops of the furniture along with brown-and-sage tweed pillows tucked against each arm.

I walked forward and couldn't help but utter, "Wow!"

Johnny stepped forward and nodded. "Yep. Incredible!"

Ryan joined us and stood on the other side of me and said, "I've been here a hundred times, but yes ma'am, that's something, isn't it? Just fucking unreal!"

He then stunned me by slapping my backside as he turned to grab our bags. I twisted with a start. Again, Johnny said nothing about the flirtatious gesture. Instead, he quietly went to the kitchen off to the right and started taking down wine glasses, and then he disappeared somewhere toward the back. I sat down on the sofa just as Ryan returned.

He came over and nodded at me. "I put your bags on the third floor in the master suite," he offered.

"Really? Well, thank you!" I said graciously. "This place is amazing."

Ryan sat down next to me and once again rested his hand on my leg. I looked down and felt uneasy.

"You know, Americans are the only ones who get all excited and say they love shit," he suddenly offered. "We're like the most enthusiastic nation! Other people say, 'Hey, I like it,' but not us, man. We *love* everything!"

I nodded and pondered that assertion. I thought he was right. Americans were excitable like that. Then Johnny reappeared in the kitchen with a bottle of wine in his hand. Ryan discretely moved his hand.

"Anyone want some wine?" asked Johnny.

"How about margaritas?" shouted Ryan who jumped up and bounced over to Johnny. He went into the kitchen and pulled out a blender, ice, Patron and margarita mix. Like a true bartender, he started blending away.

Johnny, who had opened the wine, came over and sat with me. "You want wine or margaritas?" he asked.

"Margaritas," I replied.

He smiled and sipped his wine. Ryan soon bounded over and offered me a margarita. He took a seat in the big, wide brown leather chair closest to us. We all sat and drank.

"Ryan, why didn't you invite one of your girlfriends?" I suddenly blurted out.

"Then she would think she's a girlfriend," he answered blithely with a grin.

"Oh," I replied. Then I wondered if Johnny was feeling that way about me since he invited me. The thought quickly passed because I truly didn't want to get into a relationship. I loved Kale and held out hope he would some day forgive me. In the meantime, though, I didn't plan to practice celibacy – as I was certain he was involved with Monica anyway. Just as I was thinking this, Ryan got up and fiddled with the computer.

He laughed and shouted, "I love the '80s," and the stereo connected to the computer began blaring The Police song "Synchronicity." I loved that song. We all began tossing back drinks. Since no one was driving home, we let the liquor flow freely. Before long, we were dancing to Modern English's "I'll Melt with You." I drank a margarita and took two shots of tequila, and my head was spinning. I started laughing uncontrollably, and Ryan and Johnny were dancing respectively in front and back of me. We were bumping and grinding together – all inhibitions completely trashed. Suddenly, Ryan grabbed me by the waist, swung me around and into a passionate kiss. Before I could even get my bearings, I realized I was kissing the wrong guy. Thing was, Johnny didn't move to stop it. I was drunk and laughing and kissing Ryan.

Johnny came in from behind me and moved in to whisper, "Fuck him good," and then I felt him leave.

I was confused and lost and in lust. Ryan was an excellent kisser. Before I knew it, he started pulling me onto the couch. With a swift and playful tug, he fell back and yanked me on top of him. I was dizzy, drunk and just completely in the moment. Johnny's permission had let all my inhibitions go. Ryan sat up and wrapped his arms around me as I straddled him on his lap. We kissed and kissed. He kissed down my neck to the top of my tank top, which he pulled down with his mouth and teeth to kiss the top of my breasts. I was absolutely numb and breathless and ridiculously horny and into it. It was a complete loss of abandon.

Something snapped open in me. I was going for it fully now. I reached down and began rubbing his cock. He laughed with total ecstasy and lust. He moved to help me. He grabbed the top of my hand and guided it up and down over his shaft and breathed heavily with lust and excitement. He then reached up and grabbed my tank top and tossed it off. He wrapped both arms around my chest and effortlessly undid my bra so that I was topless. He kissed and sucked my breasts. I was moaning and so into him. He was kind of crazy and fun in his lovemaking. He laughed and kissed, and then reached down and pulled off my pants in one swift maneuver. His right hand plunged down, and he smoothly stroked me, too. He then just as easily pulled off his own pants, and we were now naked with our flesh pressed warmly together. He turned forward, and I sat on him and went for a wild ride. We pushed up and down and began fucking with a crazed intensity in between his laughs and moans.

"You're fucking gorgeous!" he cried as he rolled me over onto my back and continued to make love to me.

He had great stamina, too. He kept moving over and over again with powerful thrusts that sent nothing but pleasure quivering through me. Maybe the alcohol clouded my perspective, but we had to have been going at it for a good 30 minutes, kissing and fucking, when finally he groaned and thrust even harder until he released. In a futile effort to satisfy me, he cupped his hands around my breasts and buried his mouth in them as he sucked my nipples and excited me right to the edge. I was too drunk to cum and felt somewhat frustrated. I relented and fell forward. He seemed to accept it and closed his eyes. I lay on top of him for the longest time, and we fell asleep with him still in me. I didn't give this whole situation another thought while I was in my drunken haze. Ah, but morning would be an entirely different story.

Chapter 7

I awoke alone on the sofa. Sometime in the middle of the night Ryan had left me sleeping. I could barely remember what we did – there was a fog clouding my brain. I lay on my back and stared at the enormous pine ceiling beam running down the center. I blinked and looked down – yes, I was still naked. I sat up and grabbed yesterday's clothes and started getting dressed. My head was pounding from a hangover-induced headache. I heard the back door opening and closing. I turned to find Johnny walking in and wearing swim trunks and drying his hair.

He stopped in front of me. He laughed and said, "You look like hell."

I nodded, sighed and got up. "I'm going to shower."

"You want me to leave you some Tylenol?" he asked.

I nodded and headed up the stairs all the way to the third floor. I should have felt embarrassed, but my head was pounding much too hard to care about anything. I walked into the grand master suite, which, by the way, was absolutely stunning – a four-poster bed covered in a big, fluffy burgundy-colored comforter took up most of the room, flanked by handmade pine dressers and side tables. A big armoire with a 56-inch flat screen TV sat on one wall. I had really missed out on sleeping in this amazing room with the bright morning light streaming in through the huge picture windows. I noticed my bag sat on the burgundy leather lounge chair in one corner. I grabbed it and headed for the oversized master bath, which was wall-to-wall, off-white marble with a big bathtub in one corner and a three-nozzle shower in the adjacent corner.

After I showered and felt somewhat better, I decided to face my "audience." I felt confused about Johnny since he literally handed me over to his friend. I might have been a little more proactive about this "pass" had I been right in the head and not saturated in alcohol. When I got downstairs, both Johnny and Ryan were eating breakfast at the table near the windows with the amazing lakefront view. I tentatively walked over – and they both looked right at me with grins on their faces. I didn't know what to make of it.

Johnny motioned to the head seat. "Breakfast cures most hangovers," he offered with a grin.

I sat down and looked at both of them, uncertain of what to say. The minute I sat down, I felt Johnny's hand move right under the table to my thigh. What the heck was going on? Ryan just gave me a sweet smile. No one acted uncomfortable at this table. In fact, it was quite the opposite. They both looked completely self-satisfied.

"Are we going to talk about last night?" I asked.

Ryan got up, leaned over, kissed me right on the lips, winked and asked, "Do we need to?"

He went to the kitchen and just left me there stunned.

Johnny leaned over toward me and said, "I'm good."

"Okay … " I replied as my voice trailed off in confusion.

Ryan returned to the table with a tray of buttermilk biscuits, which he slid right into the breadbasket before setting the tray back down on the counter. I reached out, grabbed one, smelled it and realized it was homemade. I immediately put it on my plate, scooped some eggs and grabbed bacon. These two guys could cook. What a strange moment. I started eating and glancing back and forth at them. They just began talking easily about the day's plans and doing some fishing later on. I realized we were staying the afternoon and decided to read onshore while they fished. No mention was made again about the confused relationships in this room.

We returned to the city late that afternoon. The boys were happy. They had caught three brown trout and planned on eating them for breakfast the next day. I was still completely thrown by this *Twilight-Zone*-like situation. Johnny had continued to act affectionately all day, touching and kissing me. Ryan, while less obvious, kissed me a few times, too. I liked them both, but this was absolutely the most bizarre triangle – and neither guy seemed the least bit bothered by it.

That evening they dropped me off in front of the apartment. I climbed the stairs and went inside. Denise was actually home, which surprised me. I put my bag down and went and sat next to her on the sofa. She was watching an HBO show called *Boardwalk Empire*.

She glanced at me. "How was your trip?"

"Bizarre ... and nice." I sighed.

"How's that?" she asked nonchalantly.

"Um, well, I don't know how to describe it. Johnny asked me to go on the trip, but Ryan, his roommate, had sex with me."

Denise's eyes grew big, and she sat up and shifted toward me. "What?"

"Don't ask me," I said with a sigh.

"Why did you screw the friend?" she asked.

"I was drunk," I replied.

"Oh, got it," she said as she laughed and nodded.

"How was your weekend?" I asked.

"Not as interesting as yours," she replied with a chuckle. Then she reached over, grabbed a note and handed it to me. "Kale called."

I looked at the note with Kale's name and number. My heart must have jumped clear up into my throat. The note said to meet him early at the office. Production was starting, and he wanted me to scout locations with him, which writers didn't usually do. I smiled. Maybe it was a peace offering. I sat back against the sofa and started mindlessly watching the show. I felt somewhat hopeful for the first time in a long time.

Chapter 8

I walked into the production offices. No one had arrived yet – it was 6:00 a.m. Most people in this industry didn't get up this early unless they were working on set. Kale's office door was wide open; I assumed to let me know to come in. I walked up and knocked on the open door. Kale was nowhere in sight. I felt a presence come up behind me. I turned around to find Kale smiling at me, and I watched his eyes scan me up and down in my white organdy sundress and flat white sandals. He handed me a latte in a Peet's cup.

"Good morning, sweetheart," he said and took a sip. "I see you got my message."

I sipped and tasted the latte – my favorite. I was touched that he remembered. "Thanks for the coffee," I said and nodded in appreciation. "I was surprised you wanted me to scout locations with you."

He looked very relaxed in khaki cargo shorts, a slate-blue T-shirt and brown leather sandals. Kale walked over and picked up a black leather backpack and talked over his shoulder as he did so, saying, "I want you to learn the entire business." He lifted the backpack and swung it over one shoulder.

"Producers don't always scout locations, but you and I will go look. Then we'll hire a production designer."

He walked out toward the front door. I trailed behind him, and a small smile slipped onto my face. It occurred to me that this was Kale's veiled way of spending time with me under the guise of work. Just as we were about to walk out into the hallway, Monica came off of the elevators. I saw a strange look on her face as she looked at both of us. I didn't know what to make of her. Was she upset or jealous? She stopped in front of Kale.

"Are you coming back in later?" she asked and moved very close to Kale, so that her line of sight was at his muscular chest. She was much shorter than my gentle giant.

"No," he replied with little emotion and walked onto the elevator that had just opened its doors.

I walked past Monica, who shifted her posture. She looked visibly troubled, and then she looked down and away from me. I ignored her and entered the elevator with Kale. It felt so good to be with him again. His presence was always a comfort to me. It was so hard not to reach out and grab his hand. He did stand very close to me, and today he didn't seem as guarded. I wasn't sure if this trip was an olive branch or just some paternal act of mentoring. I never said I intended to produce, but it occurred to me that maybe I should make it a goal.

His silver Mercedes was waiting downstairs for us with the valet. I slid into the passenger side and Kale got in the driver's seat. He turned on his iPod and Coldplay's "Glass of Water" played. Kale drove a little over the speed limit, and we zipped down the freeway. The convertible top was folded down. The wind blew through Kale's blonde hair, and the sun shone bright and luminescent on him. He looked like some ethereal, glowing god. He glanced at me and gave me the warmest smile. What had changed? He was barely talking to me last week, and here today he seemed relaxed and genuinely happy.

"You look good," I said quietly.

Kale shifted and glanced at me. "You, too," he replied and reached across the seat to stroke my upper leg. It was gentle and sweet. The moment was also deeply loaded in unexpressed emotion. So many things we had not said to each other. Was he willing to forgive me? Should I bring it up and spoil this peacefulness between us? Or could we get past it if we didn't discuss it?

We soon arrived at Highway 1 and drove north. I didn't even know where we were going. "What's first?" I finally asked.

"Malibu Lagoon," he said. "It's the big surfer spot. You have all those beach and surfer scenes. We need to look at local choices."

"Maybe I don't want to produce," I said suddenly.

Kale laughed. "You say that now."

"What's that supposed to mean?" I asked with a furrowed brow.

"It means you're working with me," he said. "I get your vision, but just one producer or director who doesn't and you'll be begging to produce."

"Why?" I ignorantly asked, eager to show him I was open to learning.

"Ask my last writer," he replied with a laugh. "You don't have the last say, Brea. Producers and directors can change your vision entirely. You end up not recognizing your own story just once — and well! You'll be begging to produce."

As the car drove over the hill, I saw the ocean and sighed – the endless blue horizon spread out in front of me. I heard Kale, and I didn't want my writing trashed. Maybe he was right. I had certainly had enough magazine editors rewrite some of my articles and not for the better. Some people just had to mark their territories and much to my chagrin.

"Are you going to trash this script?" I suddenly asked.

Kale shook his head. "No, we had you do that," he said and laughed.

"What?" I asked and frowned.

"All those rewrites." He gave me a reassuring look.

"Oh," I replied and looked down at my hands. I realized he had upset me. I had been nervously picking at my nails.

Kale glanced at the physical proof of my edginess. He frowned and reached across and rubbed my arm. "What's this?" he asked.

"Nothing," I said flatly, not wanting to address the insecure swell in the pit of my stomach. I didn't know why, but I felt completely off and anxious. Maybe it was the undercurrent of tension between us. I felt an urge to lean across and kiss him, but quickly suppressed it. I had assured myself

Kale would have to make the first move if we were to reunite. And I still felt certain – especially after running into her that he and Monica were together. I didn't want Kale to think I would ruin their relationship if it meant something to him. I just didn't know how to ask.

He pulled the Mercedes into the parking lot, killed the ignition, leaned back and grabbed his backpack. He didn't say anything and got out. He pulled his sandals off and tossed them into the backseat. He walked ahead of me and then turned and waited. I tossed my own sandals and rushed to catch up with him. He was so much taller that he walked so much faster, and it forced me (despite my own height) to hustle slightly quicker than usual to keep up with him. Kale seemed like a man on a mission. The crashing of the waves made a regular and soothing background noise. I loved the steady roar of the waves and the foaming bubble noise. He found an outcropping of rocks and began taking pictures from all angles. I figured he would give the pictures to the production designer.

After about 30 minutes, he knelt down, opened his backpack, pulled out a blue blanket and rested it in the sand. Then he pulled out Tupperware loaded with vegetables and fruits. He sat down on the blanket and looked at me expectantly. I realized we were going to picnic and sat down next to him. As I sat, he felt familiar and close. He extended a plastic bowl loaded with fresh blackberries, from which I happily took a few to eat.

"Fresh summer fruit," he said quietly and leaned back as he lazily chewed.

I nodded. "I love cherries, blackberries, raspberries."

Kale looked at me with his clear, light eyes – his eyes were at once intense and yet very expressive. "Are you still seeing the *guy?*" he asked.

I sat up a bit and looked at him, searching his face for anger. He looked interested, but relaxed. I supposed we could talk about it since he brought it up. "No, and I was not seeing him when we were together," I replied.

"No?" he said. "Didn't look that way to me," he said with a slight hint of rancor.

I knew it was now or never. "Kale, what we have — had," I corrected myself, "had nothing to do with it. Have you ever gotten involved with someone and you know it's wrong, but there is something so deeply chemical between you that it's inexplicable?"

Kale nodded a bit and then looked down. "I thought that's what we had," he said.

I moved so that I was now sitting on my knees in front of him. "No," I said flatly. "We're real!"

Kale nodded and asked, "Do you know how many nights I sat around trying to get past what you did? I want you back, but I can't trust you. How am I supposed to get over such a fundamental part of any relationship?"

"Maybe you don't force it," I said and moved up closer to him. I wanted to kiss him so badly it hurt. I deeply missed him.

His eyes met mine. He stared at me with such force. We didn't say anything at all when my phone rang in my purse. I knew I should ignore it.

"You should answer that," he said.

I picked it up and saw what it said and put it back. Kale looked at me suspiciously. "Let me see it — please."

I stared him straight in the eyes. He just unflinchingly looked back. I knew right then I would have to be transparent whether it was good or bad. If I quit hiding things, then maybe we would at least heal our friendship in some way. I handed him the phone, which was still ringing, and he saw the name. His eyes widened a moment, and then he handed it back to me. It stopped ringing.

Kale rose to his feet. I, too, stood upright. He picked up the blanket and shook the sand out. He carefully folded it and tucked it back away. Then he moved very close to me and hovered, but not in a menacing way. His eyes looked somewhat sad, but still focused as he held my gaze.

"I have to warn you, sweetheart," he said. "Unions are nasty things. That actor could take down the whole production."

He started walking back to the car. I didn't know what to say. We finally got back to the Mercedes, and each put on our respective pairs of shoes. I walked up to him and blocked his way into the car. This move stopped him in his tracks. I pressed in very close to him. He held my gaze for a moment, but seemed paralyzed by indecision. He wanted to kiss me too, but I could see the internal struggle going on by the expression on his face. I didn't want to prematurely rush anything, so I eventually relented, stepped aside and got in the passenger side. We said nothing on the drive back.

Chapter 9

A few days later, I received a strange "summons" – and when I say summons I mean command – from Curtis. He asked me to meet him at the Coffee Bean & Tea Leaf the next morning. It was how he said it on my voice mail: "Meet me at nine." No "please" or "would you" just a demand to meet him. I assumed it was business, and from the tone of his voice, it was serious business. It made me nervous, and my overly active mind went crazy with thoughts. Were they going to fire me? Replace me with another writer? Was Kale too chicken to do it himself? No, Kale was, if nothing else, respectful and decent. He wouldn't fire me that way. He would do it himself. But wait! Kale had said numerous times how I was talented and all. Why would he fire me? Maybe it was more script notes and production would be delayed. Maybe they were canceling the entire film?

"Ah stop!" I said aloud to myself alone in my bedroom.

I realized I was baking the cake, and it wasn't even in the oven. Denise had left some Ambien in her medicine cabinet. If ever I needed a sleep aid, it was tonight. She wouldn't care if I took one. So I got up in my peppermint-striped nightgown and headed to the bathroom, where I opened the cabinet, grabbed the marked prescription bottle and took a little white pill. I immediately felt my tension ease – not because of the pill, but because I knew I could now sleep. I returned to my room and the warmth of my comforter. It felt good.

I awoke suddenly and promptly at 7:00 a.m. the next day. That pill really had worked – I felt like I had closed my eyes and then opened them. Quiet and peaceful sleep had been a treat. My phone honked to indicate I had a text message. I picked it up and looked. It was from Ryan. Ryan? Now he was texting me?

"Meet me at Bardot?"

I was intrigued, smiled and asked him what time. After all, Ryan was not a production hazard. So why not meet him? He was fun, and I needed some fun.

"Late. Around 10:00?"

I said yes, and then I rushed to get in the shower. I wanted to hurry up and meet Curtis so I could find out what he had to say. I decided the best approach was to stay in the moment and see what was really going on. All this wasted worrying was killing me. I got dressed and wore a cute red sundress with a black bolero with flowers around the edges and over the shoulders. I looked chic without being too fussy. I slipped on plain, black pumps with an open toe, braided my blonde hair so that it curved over my shoulder next to my face and tied it with a sweet blue band. I wanted to stay conservative today. Curtis really made me uncomfortable.

I arrived at the Tea Leaf, and he was sitting out front

reading his Blackberry, engrossed in something. He looked up, smiled and set it down. I pulled out the iron chair, which made a scraping noise on the pavement. Curtis had two cups sitting in front of him and slid one across to me.

I looked down, smiled and asked, "For me?"

"I took the liberty of ordering hazelnut." He smiled. "I noticed you liked it."

"How sweet," I replied. "Thanks!" I said and took a sip.

Curtis looked at me with a curious tilt to his head, grinned and asked, "You have a manager?"

"No," I replied. "Kale said they're all bloodsuckers and that I should get an entertainment attorney."

"Kale said?" he asked with a strange look.

"Well, yes," I replied and frowned.

Curtis looked down at his coffee cup and seemed to weigh his response. He then carefully spoke, "I think you need a manager – someone to take you to A-list writer's status. You need someone to think ahead for you. You know, watch out for you."

"Kale watches out for me," I said plainly.

Curtis slid forward and lowered his voice. "Kale watches out for Kale. Don't be so naïve."

I sat up straight. "I'm not."

"Yes, you are," he said and stretched out his arms. "This is Hollywood, baby."

"And what's your point?" I retorted.

"My point, baby, is you need me," he said in a low voice as he slid his hand on top of my thigh.

I looked down at his hand and back up at his face. He was serious. I looked back down at that hand and cautiously slid it off. "Not sure what you're suggesting, Curtis."

Curtis moved in even closer and whispered, "You know exactly what I'm suggesting."

He sat back in his chair and had the smuggest look on his face. He was still my boss. I felt a surge of adrenaline and fear. I sat there and wasn't sure what to do or say. He could do damage no matter what. I needed him on my side, but I didn't want him on my side this way. He was eye candy that was for sure, but he was also potentially dangerous.

"I'll think about it," I replied in what seemed like a pat answer to buy me time. "But maybe you ought to woo me a little." I smiled in my own creepy way just to needle him and put him a little off-balance, too.

Curtis sat up a bit and looked at me in surprise. He laughed. "Maybe," he replied.

I took another sip of my hazelnut-flavored coffee and let it slide slowly down my throat. I looked off for a moment in the distance so I could think. Curtis grabbed his cup and briefcase and stood up. He walked partway round our little table, leaned over and kissed my cheek. He then leaned in and whispered with his hot breath right into my ear, which made the hair on the back of my neck stand on end. "Maybe," he breathed in a soft, seductive way.

I tilted away just slightly and looked up into his eyes – our eyes locked in a showdown. He leaned in and kissed my other cheek this time. I let him.

"I have a meeting," he said. "See you."

He took off and left me sitting there alone, pensive and nervous. He could hurt me. I knew that much. I could tell Kale, set off a war in the office and destroy the production that way, too. Just as I was fretting over my dilemma, I heard a terrible and familiar voice. I looked up to find Drew standing over me.

"Well, where have you been?" I asked.

Drew just took the chair across from me without asking. "Tour."

"Oh," I replied. "I forgot about that. How'd it go?"

"Going back to school," he chuckled.

Drew always said that if the band didn't work out, he would return to UCLA and pursue something else. As I looked at him, I thought I should hate him. I didn't feel hate or anger. We had a chasm between us now that consisted of space and time. I was moving on. He was apparently moving on, too. I actually, surprisingly, was happy to see him. I also felt completely at ease, which was a surprise given our last encounter where we had sex and he told me he loved me but couldn't be with me.

"Are you disappointed?" I asked.

"No," he replied. "You look good."

"Thanks." I nodded and smiled.

"Relaxed, happy," he said. "Did you get back together with that guy?"

He just had to go and spoil it. "No," I replied in a guarded tone.

Drew looked down, and I thought I saw an actual guilty look on his face. "I thought you would," he said, and now he couldn't make eye contact.

I felt my stomach tighten. I took another drink of coffee. "Hey, Drew, it's really good to see you," I said and rose.

Drew looked surprised that I was leaving and slid back a little. I grabbed my Gucci bag off the other chair. "I have to go. Work."

Drew stood up, and we were standing face-to-face. I felt a familiar attraction, but resisted. I touched his arm to say good-bye, Drew nodded and I walked off. I didn't ask him where he was working now that he was back from tour and no longer earning a living at the bikini shop – and I didn't want to know. I didn't want any more temptation or connection to him. If I saw him, I would always be respectful and kind, but the damage was done – and there could be no going back. Besides, I had far more serious things to put my attention on. Now that I had the Curtis problem brewing.

Chapter 10

I walked into Bardot and immediately spotted Ryan sitting alone in a corner, drinking what looked like gin and soda with a twist of lime. He was wearing a thin royal blue long-sleeved shirt that hugged his biceps and made me horny just looking at him. His shorn sandy-colored hair had light gel running through it. He waved me over, and I moved with a sexy sway to my hips. I was wearing a low-cut, leopard-print, long-sleeved blouse with a silver-and-cream-colored beaded choker and matching earrings.

Ryan stood right up and hugged me. I felt his warm, hard body against mine. He was handsome, rugged and built. He kissed my cheek, ordered a margarita for me (I supposed to pay homage to our tryst), and then we settled down and sat across from each other.

An awkward silence fell between us, and I finally looked down and asked, "Are you sure Johnny would be okay with this?"

"Johnny moved out," he said bluntly. "I don't give a shit what he thinks."

"What? When?" As I said this, I dared to ask what could

be construed as a major ego question. "Not because of me? I mean — I don't. Well, we aren't together."

Ryan really laughed and said, "No." He took a sip of gin and then patted the seat next to him for me to come sit closer.

I looked at where his hand landed and then back up at his cheeky smile. I relented and moved over just as the margarita arrived. Ryan moved in close and wrapped his arm around the top of my shoulders and gave me an endearing squeeze. He then released me and sat forward to take another drink.

"He accepted a part on my dad's new film and got all chummy with him – fucker," he said with seething resentment.

"What?" I asked and didn't understand.

"Johnny's a user," he spit back. "Watch out for him."

"A user?" I felt awkward with my series of questions that were clearly inciting Ryan's anger. I wasn't sure I wanted to spend the evening in "angry" discussion over cocktails.

Ryan turned toward me and suddenly leaned in to kiss me passionately – now this was preferable to an acidic, going-nowhere Q and A. "Let's not talk about them, all right?"

"Okay," I agreed.

"You want to be my girlfriend?" he suddenly asked.

I pulled away, frowned and slowly shook my head. "I don't think so. We barely know each other."

"Ah, come on, let's pretend," he said as he pulled me up to my feet and gently guided me to the dance floor. We started slow dancing to Coldplay's *Parachutes*. Our bodies were gently tangled together, swaying in perfect harmony like a tree in a soft breeze. He ran his hand down my bare back and softly moved his fingertip inward and under the edge of my dress and the very beginning of the soft mound of my breast. It was so gentle and such an erotic moment. He reached up and caressed my cheeks, and he gently moved a wisp of hair away from my face and back. The music stopped and paused before an electric dance tune I didn't recognize started. Ryan stood up and just stared at me with such tenderness. What happened to my playboy? His spirit tonight was calm and soft.

And then, being the expert at shredding a nice moment, I asked, "What happened to a new girl a night?"

Ryan's light blue eyes flickered in the light. "You like that better? Pretending over now?"

We walked back to our table and sat down. I weighed my answer and said, "Yes, I like that – and pretending … for now."

Ryan nodded and picked up his drink again. I took a sip of the margarita. When he turned back to me, his eyes were aglow with light and playfulness. "Ah, fuck it. Let's go have sex!"

Well, that was straightforward. I guess the dance was foreplay. Since a tryst with Johnny was out no matter what because he was cast in my film – and these two were no longer roommates, I decided to enjoy it. We drove in his black Range Rover straight to his house up in the Hollywood Hills. As we pulled up, a gate opened, and we drove up into a small lot with a ranch-style house sitting in the middle of trees and well-manicured flowerbeds. Ryan and I were just laughing and enjoying each other.

He parked in the driveway, jumped out and opened the door for me. I got out, and I swear we were like two little kids. He grabbed my hand and pulled me forward. He used his key, swung open the front door, turned and, like a piper, he turned and used his finger to draw me toward him in a come-to-me motion. I laughed at his silly gesture and walked into the house. It had three huge floor-to-ceiling windows, overlooking the Los Angeles basin below. It was another stunning view.

He went to the bar and poured two glasses of champagne. I sat down on the sofa and stared at the view. He walked over and handed me a glass.

"And you live off your daddy?" I asked.

"And my granddaddy," he said with a smile.

"You make no apologies?"

"Nope, I do what I want – and that doesn't bother either of them," he said frankly.

"Are you sure about that? Freeloader," I teased.

Ryan started to laugh and said, "Freeloader never! It takes hard work to be me."

I nodded and smiled. "I believe you."

Ryan leaned in and smelled me with a soft inhale and then moved in closer like he might bite me like some vampire. Instead, he kissed me softly three times up the neck. Then he pulled back and said, "I want to take you skydiving."

"What! No way!" I firmly replied. First, I was terrified of

crashing in a plane. I even once had a psychic tell me I had died in a plane crash in a previous life – and I believed him. Second, I was scared of heights. And third … well, third, I valued my life.

"Come on, Brea! You, of all the women I've met, would love it!" he chortled.

I shook my head and replied, "Really no!"

"I can change your mind," he said and suddenly grabbed my legs and pulled them up and onto the edge of the sofa. He then slithered up them like a snake on a ladder, reached under my skirt and slowly pulled off my silk thong. While he did this, he kept his eyes fixed on mine. I didn't blink and met his intensity with my own. He then moved his face up to my bush, found the right spot, and began a slow, seductive lick-and-kiss maneuver that sent a shudder throughout my body. I leaned back and let the wave of pleasure come over me. I moaned as his tongue got busier.

"Oh my god," I breathlessly stammered. I felt the tension stir and build. He was patient and talented. I moaned again, and he reached up and with impressive talent unbuttoned my blouse buttons with one hand. It quickly flashed through my mind that this guy knew his way around women's apparel too well – not to mention their body parts. I let that thought pass – this pleasurable tension was building up quickly and unbearably close to release. And then the orgasm hit fast – over and over again. I moaned in deep, uncontrolled pleasure from the powerful sensation. It had been some time since I had experienced such an intense orgasm. Darn! This guy was really good.

I sat up to kiss him. He pushed my blouse back and off. He reached around and artfully undid my black bra and pulled it off. Then he was on me again, cupping and rubbing my breasts with passion and softness all at once. He teased and played. Before I realized it, he was naked and on top of me. He kept kissing me full on the lips, with just a little tongue but not overkill. He made his way down my neck to my chest and kissed my breasts. I just wanted him in me. So, I reached down and found him aroused and ready. I pushed him inside of me, and he began to oblige my hunger by moving up and down with a passionate, perfect rhythm.

He did it on top of me for 10 minutes or so, and then he reached around, held my back and artfully flipped me on top of him to take a ride. He held my hips with his hands and guided me. I was lost in pleasure, and the alcohol now found its way into my thighs and bloodstream. I quivered a bit and felt a raw, pleasurable numbness. I sped up to give him more pleasure. He groaned, and I could actually feel him cum inside of me. This sensation turned me on so deeply that I came again right with him. I fell forward onto his chest like a puddle of relaxation and satiation.

We lay together quietly, both breathing heavily. After a few moments, we retreated to his bedroom. He lay down naked and waited for me, and then pulled me back on top of him. I sat looking down on him, smiling so happily. Ryan was an energetic, happy-go-lucky guy. I didn't feel any need to assign any complexity to it. I had no idea if we would hook up again now or later or ever – and that was okay. I had not lost track of my desire to right things with Kale.

"You're fun," I suddenly offered as a compliment.

Ryan sighed. "And you would be more fun if you would go skydiving with me."

"I said no," I replied and fell off him and onto the bed.

"Come on, Brea, it's unreal. You will feel nothing like it in the world."

"You know what? You get a job, and I'll go skydiving," I replied.

"Why do you want me to get a job so bad?" he asked.

"You can't possibly think that this is satisfying?" I objected.

Ryan rolled over on his side and looked at me. "*This* is very good!" he said as he reached and caressed my breast.

I looked down, smiled and nodded. "Yes, but *this* gets boring fast!"

"Not with you," he countered and then leaned forward to kiss me. He gently grabbed my hand and pulled it down to cover his hard bulge. He was ready so quickly. I obliged and pulled him on me for round two. And it was just as great as round one.

Chapter 11

The next day, Kale summoned me to the office – early again. He said he wanted to talk about something important. When I arrived, he was dressed in a button-down, light-blue, short-sleeved shirt that matched his eyes and jeans. He looked happy to see me. We seemed to be making progress – our relationship had mellowed into a comfortable ambiguity.

It felt so warm and nice to be around him that I thought I would take what time I could get alone with him and enjoy it. I also suspected he called me in early to ensure quality alone time before the staff arrived. It seemed like Monica had made it her habit lately to interrupt us. I didn't know if Kale had noticed, but I sure had. I had completely avoided any discussion that would define their relationship because I held out hope that their intimate closeness was in my imagination. A California girl could hold out hope anyway.

Kale walked straight over to me and hugged me. To my utter shock, he leaned over and gave me a simple, but sweet kiss on the lips, not the cheek. I was completely blown away by the simplicity of what amounted to an intimate gesture. Yes, I knew our relationship had progressed well beyond kisses, but there was a familiar tenderness to it and certainly no seduction behind it.

"Hey," I said as I pulled back with a surprised look on my face.

"Let's do something fun," he said.

"Fun?" I asked. "Not work? Why?"

Kale sat down on the edge of his desk, crossed his legs and shrugged. "We did a lot of things backward," he admitted. "I thought about it. Who was I to assume I knew who was in your life?"

I stepped forward and said, "I didn't exactly tell you."

"True, sweetheart, you didn't, but I don't recall asking either," he said. "My bad."

"Are you forgiving me?" I asked as my heart started beating quickly.

Kale just stared at me with those strong, bottomless eyes I loved so much. "Not sure," he said simply. "I do want to know you, though. I want to spend real time with you."

I grinned and said, "Not just my body?" I moved forward a little closer and cocked my head in a flirtatious way.

"Brea, you are the most gorgeous woman I know. I also realize you can have any man you want when you want. Do I want your body? That's not even a question," he said with a quiver of a grin. "I could seduce you now – maybe not even regret it, but where did that get me last time? So no, not your body ... for now."

I reached out and lightly touched his bicep. His eyes drifted down to the touch and then back up. He stood up, which forced me to drop my touch. "What I want is your time."

"To do what?" I asked.

"Just time, sweetheart," he said. "I own a boat. We're going out to catch fresh fish off the bow. I'm going to cook it for your dinner," he said and started to walk toward the door where he stopped and waited.

"What if I said I get seasick?" I asked.

"Well, then, sweetheart, we'll stop and get you Dramamine," he said in his silky voice and opened the door. "After you."

I hesitantly walked toward the door, stopped right in front of him, gazed into his eyes and smiled. What I saw was acceptance of some sort. This gesture, this quasi-date was a test of some kind – I felt it. Was he going to forgive me? He said he was uncertain. Would he ever forgive me? The answer was as vague as the gesture. I reached the quick conclusion that my lesson for the week was about staying in the moment and accepting it for what it was.

We strolled out into the hallway and ran smack into Curtis, who looked from Kale to me and asked, "Where are you two going?"

"Boating," said Kale, unaffected by the question.

"With her?" he asked as if I was not standing there.

Kale's eyes drifted to me and back to Curtis. "And your point?"

Curtis raised his hand with the coffee cup in it. "No, man; no point. Have fun."

And as Curtis walked past me I felt his eyes shift down on

me. I could sense jealousy and a hint of anger. It made me uncomfortable. Kale also looked from Curtis to me. We walked to the elevator and got in it.

Kale turned to me and said, "I've known him for years. Good guy. Does he bother you?"

"Um — no," I said and deflected the truth.

"You have nothing to worry about with him. All bark, I promise," he said. "Because you would tell me?"

"Tell you?" I asked flatly.

Kale eyed me suspiciously and then shrugged. "All right, sweetheart, you play it that way."

Shit! Every time I came close to true intimacy, something ruined it. I wasn't sure if Kale was upset, suspicious, frustrated or what. I saw his expression become more guarded again. I wanted to tell him the truth, but it seemed like a reckless choice – one that would ultimately shut down production on my first film. This industry was littered with films that almost were – and movie shutdowns were often instigated by far less trivial problems than a rivalry over the screenwriter. If I told Kale, he might protect me but at what cost? Could my career afford that kind of protection? And, with our romantic relationship still questionable, was now the right time? Maybe Kale would tire of the sexual drama that I seemed to invite.

Later that morning, we arrived at a dock in San Diego at the marina. We walked out on the long wooden planks that had boats moored on each side like parked cars. The gentle breeze blew cool air and pushed my hair back. I reached in my bag, pulled out a band and tied my hair back off my face.

It felt good. Kale came to a sudden stop in front of me, and I turned and looked. This was the "boat"? It was a yacht with wide-open windows on the upper deck. I looked up and stared, and I'm sure my surprise registered on my face.

Kale chuckled. "You weren't expecting a rowboat were you?"

"No," I replied with a smile, "but I wasn't expecting a yacht either!"

One of the deckhands was waiting for us on the boat. Kale reached down and helped me up on the plank between the dock and the boat. I took his hand (it felt good) and allowed his assistance. He turned and whispered something to the deckhand, who disappeared and reappeared a few minutes later with a glass of water and two pills in an outstretched, white-gloved hand.

"What's this?" I asked.

"Dramamine," he responded.

I took the water and tossed the pills in my mouth just as Kale turned to look at me. He had a weird expression on his face.

"What?" I asked.

"Nothing." He grinned. "I'll meet you up on deck, all right?"

He headed off to the front of the boat with the deckhand and disappeared into a room. I looked around, spotted some stairs just inside the main cabin and made my way up them to the upper deck. As I emerged through the top, I saw the view of the open sea out off the stern. It was incredible – blue and clear. The water shimmered and rippled in the midday sun.

The sea breeze blew and swirled through my hair. I heard the engine rumble and start. I looked over the edge and saw two more deckhands undoing the ropes and tossing them on board. I sat down in a plush, beige chair with a round table separating it from a matching chair. Just as I looked up, a steward appeared in front of me holding out a tray containing champagne, cheese and fruit.

"Miss," he said quietly.

I grabbed the champagne by the stem, took a small plate of grapes and cheese and set both down on the small, round table next to my seat. My phone chirped to alert me of a text. I pulled it out of my purse and looked – it was Lance. He asked to see me later. I replied maybe and put the phone away. I wasn't sure what time we would return. I was worried about Lance. He said the chemo was terrible, but he wouldn't share much more than that. I suddenly felt guilty being so preoccupied with my own petty concerns when Lance was so sick. And I hadn't been a good friend to him at all. I needed to step up.

Kale emerged from below and came to sit next to me. "Have you ever gone deep-sea fishing?"

"No, not really," I said. "I fished for trout in a river with my sister when I was little."

"Oh, you have a sister?" he asked.

"Her name is Lulu, and she lives in northern California. We're not close."

Kale nodded and smiled. "Maya loves you," he said frankly. "She wants us back together – tells me every morning," he said with a laugh.

I looked at him and leaned across the table. "So do I," I said and popped a grape into my mouth.

Kale leaned in closer and looked at me. "You fucked us up," he said briskly.

I sat up straight. "Yes, I did."

Kale looked at me. "An honest answer. Now we're getting somewhere."

I looked down and then took another sip of champagne. "In my defense, it was just … I don't know — unexplainable. Haven't you done something like that before?"

Kale picked up a pair of binoculars and started looking at something off in the distance. "Two whales," he said and handed the binoculars to me and pointed off to the south.

I took the binoculars and looked. Yes, two whales. They were merely ripples under the water, but I could see their spray from their blowholes sending up water like a fine mist in the air. I handed the binoculars back and sipped more champagne. He wasn't going to answer that question.

"You don't think I'm honest?" I suddenly asked.

Kale, who had returned to gazing through the binoculars, took them down from his eyes, raised an eyebrow and sort of smirked. "Do you think you're honest, sweetheart?"

I shifted back into my seat and looked down at my hands. I considered that question very carefully. "I didn't lie … exactly."

"That's not what I asked you." He looked me right in the eyes.

"It's not lying if I just didn't mention what was going on. And I never said I loved you." As I said those words, I could see pain cross Kale's face. I suddenly wished I could grab the words and shove them back in the proverbial bottle. Wrong answer.

Kale got up, grabbed his champagne and finished it off in one full gulp. He wouldn't look at me anymore. "I'm going fishing. You joining me?"

I stood up and said, "I'll watch."

Kale and I walked down to the bottom of the ship and to the back. A deckhand was waiting with a huge fishing rod. Kale immediately worked to put giant-sized fish chunks on it as bait. I found my way to a cushy bench nearby. As I sat in the warm light of day, rocking with the soft, gentle sway of the boat, my eyes grew heavier and heavier. I thought it was the champagne. Within minutes, I realized I could barely hold my eyes open. Kale was busily fishing. So, I thought I would lie down on the bench and just close them – that was the last thing I remembered.

The next thing I knew my eyes were open – and it was sunset. Kale was standing over me in all his tallness, nudging me awake and laughing. "Brea! Wake up. Dinner."

"Huh," I whispered and forced my eyes open. "What?"

I pulled myself up, and Kale reached out and grabbed my hand to steady me. "You all right?"

"I couldn't keep my eyes open," I explained.

Kale softly laughed and looked out on the horizon and then back. "Dramamine, sweetheart. I tried to warn you, but you just took both pills at once."

"Oh, what? I don't understand," I replied.

"It causes drowsiness," he replied, and we started up the staircase back to the top and the dining area.

When we got to the deck, I noticed the table was perfectly set with every piece of silverware and glassware in its proper place. The deckhand pulled out my chair for me. Kale sat across from me. His cheeks were a nice shade of rosy red from being in the sun, which made his eyes look even bluer than usual. He looked so relaxed and satisfied. He told me he caught white sea bass, which we were having for dinner. It sounded so succulent and fresh. The deckhand poured another glass of champagne as we spoke of the afternoon that I had managed to miss in my sleep. Kale was deliriously happy about the adventure. He said he saw so many whales it was unreal and even a breech. I'd never seen a man so happy to describe a breech in my life. He said it was a huge tail that came up vertically and than flat down with an amazing splash. He ate his fish with contentment, and you would think he was angler of the year.

"Do you really think I'm a liar?" I asked quietly, eating my fish.

Kale took a bite, chewed and considered his answer. "No, I think you're young," he admitted.

"Immature?" I asked and dreaded the answer.

"You're extremely focused, talented, kind and, of course, easy on the eyes," he said and smiled at me. "I never once thought you intended to hurt me."

"I'm immature then?"

Kale's expression softened into a sweet, paternal look. "You're weak. I don't dislike that about you exactly. But you're also vulnerable – and that is a beautiful thing, especially here in La La Land," he said mockingly. "The first time we met, and I offered to put you in the movie and you instantly declined, I knew you were well beyond anyone in that room."

I grabbed my champagne glass and took a swig. I felt really bad. The subtext of this conversation was creating a pit in my stomach. I could hear the imaginary "but" without him actually saying it. All I wanted to do was reach across the table, clear the plates and dishes and have fantastic out-to-sea sex; but I could see by his tender expression and the subtext that it was not going to happen – not tonight.

"By the way, who's Ryan?" he asked.

"What?" I asked, surprised he knew about Ryan.

"He texted you 10 times. I looked," he admitted.

I was uncomfortable. I didn't know if I liked his snooping on my iPhone. "I'm seeing him," I said frankly. After all, I was certain Kale was involved with Monica. Why would I not be seeing someone else? We weren't together anymore.

"I see," he said. "And what about Johnny? Aren't those two friends?"

"I was never involved with Johnny," I said and thought at least this answer might make him happy.

"Hmm ... " he said and looked me straight in the eyes. "Are you fucking Ryan?" he asked with this unsettling intensity.

"Yes," I replied bluntly.

"Honesty … twice in one afternoon. Impressive."

"Ryan is fun. He's not you. I would be with you if you wanted me," I said.

Kale looked up, set down his fork and moved closer to me. He leaned in very close to my face so that I could smell his scent – fish, peppermint and just Kale. It was a mixture that was not displeasing. Nothing about Kale was disappointing. He grabbed my hand and gently placed it on his substantial and familiar manhood and smiled.

"I never said I didn't want you," he whispered.

I felt a surge of heat well up into my thighs. I met his gaze with the same intensity, but right then he pulled away and out of my space. I felt a jolt of shock mixed with intense lust and longing. Kale gripped the champagne bottle chilling on ice and poured my glass back full to the top and topped his own off. He smiled his captivating grin, reached out with his glass to suggest cheers and took a brisk drink. I sat back in my seat, stared at him and took my own sip. I was completely enthralled with him.

"We'll be back at dock by 8:00 p.m. Your friend Lance wants you to come by at 8:30. I texted him and said I would have you back in time."

What? Now I was reeling in shock. I looked down. What was he doing? Messing with me? I didn't really know. "I'm — I'm not sure you should have done that," I said quietly.

Kale stiffened a bit. "I want to trust you again."

"But that's my private phone," I replied.

"Well, then I'll try not to look at it from now on," he replied and looked me straight in the eyes.

"You have no idea how much I want you," I suddenly blurted out and admitted.

Kale sweetly smiled out of nowhere and said, "Good."

I kept staring at him, but he made no move toward me. I backed down and concentrated on my food for the rest of the evening. He wasn't going to make this easy.

Chapter 12

After I bid Kale good-bye, I headed straight to Lance's apartment. I was very worried about him. He had never specifically asked to see me before, so I knew something was up. When I got there, a bald caregiver opened the door. I was alarmed just by his presence. He said his name was Jim and that Lance was on the patio. I had to steel myself – it had to be bad if he had a caregiver at the apartment. So I walked to the sliding door that was cracked open already and peered out through it. The sight of Lance asleep on the chair with a blanket pulled all the way up to his chin and a blue dew rag on his head to cover his now bald scalp was alarming. I sucked in air. I had to go out there, try to look calm and not allow him to see the shock on my face.

I carefully stepped out onto the patio and quietly pulled up a chair next to the white chaise lounge. He was asleep, and I could hear his quiet breathing. I didn't want to wake him up and decided to sit with him for a while. I looked out over the skyline aglow with the city lights. It was a warm, peaceful night. I could hear the freeway noise buzzing off in the distance and Lance's steady inhaling and exhaling.

Soon Jim poked his head out and said, "He wanted to see you." Then he handed me a small white cup of pills. "Here, wake him and give him these," he requested and extended a glass of water with the other hand.

I nodded and took the pills and glass. I turned back to Lance, set down the two items on the small table between us and nudged him with the soft tip of my finger. "Hey, you," I whispered. "You need to take your meds."

Lance's eyes slowly fluttered open; he saw me and gave me the warmest smile. "Brea," he whispered like a happy little boy who just saw his mother at his side.

"Your meds," I said again and handed them over.

He brought his thin arms from beneath the blanket and took the pills and glass of water. He tossed the pills into his mouth and took a big drink. He set the two items down and shifted toward me. "You look pretty," he whispered and smiled, satisfied with the sight.

I felt sunburned and tired. "You're a sweetie, you know that?"

Lance kind of lightly laughed. "I wanted to see you."

"I know," I replied. "You spoke to Kale."

"Yeah, you know, Brea, he's a good guy," Lance said with a gentle smile of approval. "You ought to work that one out."

"Not up to me," I replied and shrugged. "How are you doing?"

"Not so good," he replied. "This disease is a fucker!" he said with more energy. "I'm tired and sick – and that's that." I leaned over and kissed him softly on the lips. His eyes widened a bit and he grinned. "How I wish I felt better."

I started to laugh and said, "Of course you do."

We sat together for the next hour talking about nothing important. Lance said he just wanted to laugh with someone. I didn't dare ask about his prognosis. He looked terrible, but it was part of the treatment. It started getting late, so I grabbed my purse to leave when Lance suddenly took my arm, pulled me into a deep, passionate kiss and drifted away. He stared at me with such intensity, I had to look away – it made me uncomfortable.

"If I die," he said, "I want you to know you are the love of my life."

"What?" I broke down in tears. "Lance … " my voice cracked and trailed off.

"Don't cry," he pleaded. "It's a beautiful thing."

I fell back in my chair, stared long and hard at him and then just lost it completely. I shook my head, kept crying and got up. "I need to go," I managed to say through sobs.

I looked at him one more time; he gave me a weak smile. I took off out the sliding door and left the apartment before Jim could see my face drenched in tears. I got in the car and just cried and cried. I sat in my car until the phone ringing made me stop crying. I looked down: It was Ryan. I wiped my tears, sniffed and picked up.

"Yeah, hey," I said.

"What are you doing?" he asked.

"Nothing," I replied curtly.

"Can you meet me?" he asked.

"It's super late," I said.

"Come on, it will be fun," he said.

I pulled the phone away from my ear, glanced at the time and said, "All right. I'll see you soon."

A short time later, I arrived at Ryan's Hollywood Hills home. He was standing out front, loading gear into his Rover. He stopped and waited for me to park and get out. I walked over and just stood there, looking expectantly at him.

"Okay, I'm here," I continued, "what?"

Ryan walked right into my space, pulled me into a hug and then kissed me passionately. "Get in," he said and stepped away.

"Why?" I asked skeptically.

"You'll see. Just get in," he commanded.

I looked from his playful eyes to the car and back again. He had the most mischievous grin on his face. Resisting the grin would be a problem. Finally, I relented and climbed in the passenger's side. After the day and evening I just had, I could use some fun. He started the engine, and we were soon on the highway, driving north to what, after a while, looked like some desert area outside of Barstow. Ryan wouldn't tell me where we were going.

It was dark, but there was no mistaking the sign that read "California Skydiving." My jaw dropped, and I shifted toward Ryan and raised my voice in protest and cried, "No way!"

Ryan pulled the car through, nodded in an overly dramatic way and laughed. "Way!"

"You can't make me!" I yelled.

Ryan pulled up in front of a brightly lit building. "We're going at night, too!" he beamed. "You won't be able to see anything but the lit targets."

He pulled into the parking space, jumped out and went to the back to unload. I stayed firmly planted in my seat with my arms folded. I had no intention of getting out of that seat to jump out of an airplane. An African-American gentleman walked out of the metal building and greeted Ryan. It was he who came around to my door and opened it. I sat firmly.

He extended his hand and said, "I'm Reddy." He grinned. "I'll be your instructor."

Ryan walked around and stood next to Reddy with his arms folded and leaned in to him. "She needs some scotch." As he said this, he reached in his coat's inside pocket and pulled out a flask, which he outstretched to me. I looked from it to him and sat in silence.

"Ah, come on, Brea, grow some hair on your chest," he encouraged.

"Yeah, Brea," Reddy goaded.

I begrudgingly grabbed the bottle from Ryan, opened the lid, took a huge swig and then clenched my teeth together in reaction to the strong liquor taste. I sat there a moment more and thought about Lance. I thought about living in the moment. Lance hadn't done much in his short life. I was sure he had regrets. Did I want to have regrets? Would this even be a fun sport I had missed out on? I didn't even have skydiving on my bucket list. Then I thought about fear. Ryan did this all of the time – and here he was alive and kicking and doing just fine.

I finally talked myself into it and slid out of the car, which caused Ryan endless delight. He grabbed me by the waist and yanked me in for a playful kiss as he bent me backward and planted yet another sweet kiss on my lips. He helped me stand back up erect and let out a loud, "Yee-haw! All right."

I went through the instruction process with Reddy in about an hour. I realized I was going to be connected to Reddy and doing nothing more than going along for the ride, which was completely fine by me. So we suited up and got on the little plane with its whirling propellers just waiting for its passengers, which to my utter chagrin included me.

I climbed into the plane with overwhelming nervousness and trepidation. I had been nursing the scotch, though, all throughout the evening. By the time I got in the airplane and took a seat on the nearest bench, I was feeling warm and tipsy. Ryan sat on my right, and I leaned into him laughing. He looked at me and smirked.

"You drunk?" he asked.

I showed him an inch between two fingers. "A little," I replied and burst out laughing.

Ryan grinned and shook his head. Reddy came over to me and sat down and said, "In about two minutes, I'm going to have you stand and I'll rig you up."

"Okay," I giggled.

Reddy frowned and looked at Ryan and asked in a loud voice so he could be heard over the roar of the engine, "Is she okay?"

Ryan waved him off. A couple of minutes later, Reddy

firmly grabbed me by the harness on the front of my red jump-suit and pulled me to my feet. I was a rag doll in his grip as he yanked, pulled, pushed and harnessed. I was so numb with fear and from the alcohol pulsing in my veins that I just flopped around as he pulled me toward the hatch. I heard a loud scream of excitement since my back was to Reddy's – it was Ryan going first.

He was screaming, "Woo-hoo!"

Reddy stepped toward the hatch, and I backed up along with him. I quickly closed my eyes determined not to look down. I felt a tug and a hard, brisk flow of air slapping my body – and away we went, free falling through the night air. I let out the most ear-piercing, high-pitched scream anyone had ever heard. I could hear Reddy and somewhere off in the distance Ryan – and both men were laughing.

"Open your eyes," screamed Reddy.

I tried to talk myself into it. I slowly let one eye open, and I could only see darkness all around and tiny dotted lights below. It was cold as the air flowed against my body. The adrenaline kicked in, and I just lost it, laughing crazily with exhilaration as I realized I was just falling. This went on for what felt like a half hour but was rapid and swift as we neared land. I felt a release of excitement and just let it all go. I felt free, thrilled and infinitely happy. We landed on the ground, and Reddy quickly released me from my harness.

I turned and saw Ryan off in the distance, yowling with excitement and laughter. Once released from my parachute, I ran off into his arms. He hugged me and lifted me up and off the ground. "Yeah," he cried and set me down. He grabbed my face and kissed me with such passion.

I pulled away. "O-M-G!" I uttered in astonishment.

Ryan looked up and yelled, "Hey, Reddy! Meet us back at the airfield."

Reddy waved us off. Ryan turned back to me and rapidly unzipped my jumper. He reached inside and grabbed both ends of my bra and unlatched it. Then he pushed up my bra and began massaging my breasts as he kissed me and wouldn't stop. We fell to the brown grass, with Ryan on top of me. He was completely hard and passionate and almost crazy with lust. I kept kissing him and responding – my mind just buzzing with electricity, adrenaline, lust and fear that transformed into excited passion. Within minutes, he managed to unzip his own suit and pull out his hard cock.

He pushed my suit off and down, and we rolled so I was on top. I began riding him with a quickened pace of exhilaration. He sat up so we formed a V and kissed me up my neck until we were nearly in a frenzy of lust, sweat and hunger for each other. Even in my numb state, I was excited as Ryan reached down and found my pleasure spot and rubbed. I was now just beside myself and besieged by ecstasy. I had never felt anything so frenetic and feverish in my life. I kissed him and wouldn't stop. He moaned, and I could feel him release into me, which got me off at the same time.

When we were done, we lay there side by side in the grass, looking up at the full moon over our heads. "I have never done anything like that in my life," I said as ripples and quivers shivered over my body.

Ryan laughed and sat up. “Fuck!” he yelled out with a scream. He turned, leaned over, kissed me and said, “Fuck, you’re hot!”

I sat up and pulled my jumpsuit back up. “Unforgettable,” I uttered.

Ryan stood up and pulled his own suit back on and said, “Let’s go home and fuck in the Jacuzzi.”

And he reached down and grabbed my hand to pull me up. And off we went together, arm in arm, happy and ready to continue as he suggested – in the Jacuzzi.

Chapter 13

When I got home the next morning, I arrived just as Denise was getting ready to leave with her briefcase in hand. She was dressed in an eggplant-colored suit and looked nice. She stopped and looked annoyed at me.

"Some jerk-off keeps calling here and hanging up," she complained. "Woke me up three times at three o'clock in the morning."

"Really? That sucks," I replied with a frown.

Denise rolled her eyes. "I have to go," she said as she headed out the front door. "And I'm not even going to ask what you were doing."

I went to shower and change. Just as I got out of the shower, I heard my iPhone chirp to alert me about a text message. I held the towel up as I grabbed it and looked – it was Maya. She told me to meet her at Kale's house after work. I was surprised, but then again Kale knew about our friendship. I hadn't been to Kale's house since we broke up. I told her I would be there and decided to work from home that day. I was writing a new script and production was starting in a few more weeks on my current movie. I wanted to get something else done and sold while I waited to be called on set to do rewrites.

After a full day's work, I went out to meet Maya at Kale's house. I pulled up in my Corolla, leaned out the window and pushed the gate button. The gates swung open, and I pulled up into the front of the Spanish-style villa that was so familiar, it made me miss Kale even more. I got out of the car and before I could go anywhere, Maya swung the door open and rushed out to greet me. She grabbed me in a boisterous hug.

"Hey, you." I smiled as she grabbed my hand and led me toward the house.

"Como estás?" she asked and smiled.

"Muy bien," I responded using my little knowledge of Spanish. She walked with me into the kitchen area and then threw a super cute gold bikini at me. "Kale bought this for you," she said. "Meet us outside."

"Us?" I asked.

Maya winked at me, stood up on her tips toes with excitement and fell back down, grabbed a strawberry from the fruit tray and disappeared through the sliding door to the patio. I looked down at the bikini and wondered if my nether regions were bikini-ready or not. I couldn't remember the last time the hedges were trimmed. I went to the bathroom and disrobed. All was good, so I got ready and grabbed the white robe hanging on the back of the door that I assumed was for me.

I stepped out onto the patio to find my blonde man-candy sitting under the shade of an umbrella, drinking champagne and talking on the phone. His eyes came to rest on me, and he sweetly nodded and smiled to acknowledge my presence. I quietly came over and sat down. I looked down into the pool – Maya was floating on a raft with her dark hair already wet and loose as she drifted around completely relaxed with her arms hanging off the sides. Kale mumbled a non-answer into the phone, said good-bye, hung up, sighed and looked at me.

"Well hello, sweetheart," he said in his silky voice. "Come round, give me a kiss."

I smiled and obliged, planting a tender kiss on his rose-petal-shaped mouth. It felt warm and loving. He looked up at me with an affectionate, sweet gaze of appreciation. "You look ... radiant?" he asked me quizzically.

"You won't believe what I did," I replied and sat down close to him.

"Oh, it's you – I'll believe it," he said and smiled.

"I went skydiving," I confessed with a huge smile on my face.

Kale shifted and sat back a little. "Did you?" He was clearly entertained by the notion. "Good for you. And how was it?"

"Amazing, scary, crazy," I responded.

Just as I said this, Curtis emerged from the house. I looked up in surprise to see him. He fixed his gaze right on me. Kale stood up, and they gave each other the half-man-hug.

"Hey, man," said Curtis.

"You, of course, know Brea – and that caramel sundae in the pool is the luscious Maya, my friend and housekeeper."

I wondered if Kale knew that Maya preferred "strawberry" sundaes in the form of women to men. Did they talk about those things? I didn't know and was not going to address it right now. And here was creepy, but gorgeous, Curtis sitting super close to me now. He was already in his swimsuit. I supposed we were all going to swim together at this impromptu gathering.

"Hey, Brea," Curtis said as his eyes drifted down to the gape in my robe that exposed my cleavage.

"Brea here just went skydiving," said Kale.

"Fuck, really?" said Curtis in astonishment. "I've always wanted to go."

Kale grabbed an orange from a nearby fruit tray and started peeling it. "Maybe Brea will teach us both. Huh, sweetheart, what do you say?"

"Um, no," I replied. "I'm not planning to do it again. Once was fine."

Kale finished peeling the orange, leveled his gaze at me and then handed the freshly peeled orange to me. I accepted the gesture and proceeded to break it apart. Kale smiled and sipped his champagne while keeping his eyes fixed on mine. I tucked a slice in my mouth – I was surprisingly hungry.

"Brea, you given any thought to that manager?" Curtis suddenly asked as he stood up and stretched to show off his cut abs, which I had to admit were stunning.

But my gaze stayed fixed on Kale's intense stare, and I avoided looking at Curtis and replied, "No."

"Well, fucking A," he yelped, jumped up and sprinted toward the water to jump in. He splashed and disturbed Maya, who upon his breaking the water's surface splashed him in the face.

"Perro!" she yelled at him.

I didn't hear his response. Kale and I were eye-fucking each other as I ate my orange slices one at a time. Kale just looked, once again, contented and mellow. "I ate fish for lunch today," he said with a sigh.

"Why am I not surprised?" I asked.

"What do you mean, sweetheart?"

"You catch a sea bass and you're like the happiest guy in the world," I smirked. "It's a fish, not Moby Dick," I said and tossed an orange peel at him playfully.

"You want to swim?" he asked.

I put my foot up on the edge of his chair very near his junk and scooted my toe right up to the tip of his head, but he didn't flinch. He kept his eyes fixed on mine. He tilted his head strangely to the side, squinted and asked, "With whom did you skydive with?"

I lowered my foot, looked down and answered him. "Ryan."

"Ryan … you know I know Ryan's daddy," he said with scorn. "He pulled financing on my first film. We were already in preproduction, and he pulled the plug. Not my favorite guy, Ry-Ry's dad."

I slid forward, leaned in toward him, arched my eyebrows and said, "One word and no more Ry-Ry."

Kale looked down, got up, disrobed and revealed his incredible, hard, cut body in all of its tall leanness. I sucked in my breath, and my eyes drifted up from bottom to top – supple, muscular, completely perfect. I decided he had to be the most handsome, perfectly proportioned man I had ever laid eyes on. I quickly matched his move by doing the same – off came the robe, which I dropped onto the chair. Kale took in the same measure of my body and gazed at me with such insane pleasure as his lips turned into a slight smile and his blue-green eyes fluttered a bit.

"I miss that body," he said plainly and honestly.

I smiled warmly, grabbed his hand and then I pulled him, and we both ran for the water. We jumped in one bound straight in and came to the surface together. Curtis had already grabbed a raft and was floating quietly near Maya. I started laughing and did the breaststroke over to Maya and rested my elbows on her raft. She opened one eye, smiled in approval and closed her eye again. I looked around to find Kale and didn't see him. All of a sudden I felt the raft rise up, and Kale had come under it to lift Maya up into the air and toss her off. She swore some choice Spanish expletives, and splashed as she fell underwater. When she came back up, she began continuously splashing Kale, who splashed right back until they were both breathlessly laughing like two little kids.

I procured Maya's raft and was watching the fight in amusement when Curtis floated over. I looked at him and had to refrain from giving him a dirty look. Now even his energy near me was a turnoff.

"You really should think about my offer," he said in a low voice. "You give me a little, I get you a lot," he said, winked and stroked away from me.

I became quiet, got off the raft, and swam over to the steps to sit and watch the group. Maya and Kale were talking about something and laughing. Curtis made his way next to Maya's raft, and they were all talking. I couldn't hear them through the steady din of the waterfall in the background. I kind of stretched out on the stairs to just watch and enjoy some peace. As usual, Curtis unsettled me. I saw Kale do a double take, and he smiled at me and swam over. He sat down very close to me on the step and sprawled out with his long muscular legs spread out in front of him. I looked at those legs and sighed.

"What's that about?" he asked.

"Your hotness," I replied.

Kale chuckled. "You're worse than a guy."

I leaned in close to him and whispered in his ear, "I sure am."

He really started laughing over that and wrapped his arm around my waist and pulled me up onto his lap. He gently lifted my wet hair up and away and began kissing me on the back of my neck. I felt the hair all over my body stand up, and I quietly leaned back against his shoulder so I was resting on him like a lounge chair. I watched Maya and Curtis swim off to the other side and exit the pool. I assumed they wanted to give us some privacy. Maya smiled the broadest, toothy smile as she passed us – and Curtis walked sullen behind her. As soon as they were both out of sight, I twisted my head just slightly and reached up and pulled him into the most passionate kiss. God, it felt great to kiss him again.

We rested there for about five minutes just kissing until I managed to reposition myself so I had my legs straddled around his waist. He was definitely hard and wanted me, but just when I might have suggested we retire to his bedroom, he stopped kissing me and looked at me with such a sweet, fond gaze.

"Sweetheart, I miss you – and I know you miss me, but we're not going to do this again," he said.

"Really?" I asked and kissed him gently. "Are you sure?"

Kale reached around, and I felt his hand go down my back. I arched forward into him. He kissed me one more time and softly whispered, "Yes."

"I'm not going to betray you again," I promised. "That's over."

"No, you're not," he said and kissed me. "I want you to be sure. I want you to look me in the eyes and say you love me."

I stared at him. His hand continued to wander up and down my back. He reached around and pulled my bikini top aside and began kissing my breasts. I was so frustrated, but he was right. I couldn't say it. I felt it, and I was immobilized. I knew if I said it, I was permanently off the market. I could not betray him ever again. It would be serious because there would be no backsliding or uncertainty. He would never again compromise on something as important as fidelity, and we would breakup for the last time. And with that I couldn't tell him. I needed the same certainty he needed – and I wasn't that clear yet. He moved up and kissed me passionately again, and the kissing went on. It felt amazing, sensual and loving. He reached up and ferociously and passionately massaged my breasts harder, and then I felt completely about to lose it. He seemed to feel the same way, so he stopped and stared at me. He pulled back.

"We better go," he said.

I grabbed his hand before he could move and met his gaze straight on. "Kale, when I tell you what I feel, it will make us real!"

He steadied himself back to maintain my look, and he nodded with such sincerity and smiled. "Ah, my sweetheart ... "

Then he got up, extended his hand to help me up and gently pulled me forward up the steps. He looked around and adjusted his situation so he didn't walk up the patio with a raging hard-on. I laughed at him. He turned and pushed my arm like he used to do.

"You dirty, dirty girl," he said and then wrapped his arms around me.

"And you love it!" I replied.

"Yes, I do."

Chapter 14

The next day, I went into the office to pick up a few things and attend some production meetings. I had intended to go straight to Kale's office to greet him. I felt really great about last night. We were making steady progress, but it wasn't loaded with too much pressure. He wasn't asking me to stop my life, and he was definitely giving me a wide berth to deliberately figure out my next move. In the meantime, I was still going to see Ryan, who was all about living life to the fullest and on the edge. Ryan didn't seem to have any expectations about what we were or were not. He was a free spirit, and right now that suited me fine.

I glided in the front door, greeted Erin who was answering the phones and started toward Kale's office only to find the door closed. I stopped and hesitated just as the door plunged open and out Monica stomped. She stopped dead in her tracks and glared at me. I was confused. She was holding the black binder or the "bible," as we called the master script, against her chest. She didn't do much more than glare at me and take off toward her office. I slowly walked into the doorway and stood there. Kale was hunched over his desk, touching some icon on his iPad.

"Hey," I said quietly.

Kale looked up, and he looked agitated. His entire mood shifted in a positive way the minute he saw me. He sat back in his chair and waved me in. "Close the door," he requested.

I stepped forward, closed the door behind me and grinned at him. He then rolled back from his desk, got up and strode toward me with a seductive look on his face. He stood right in front of me, wrapped his arms all the way around my waist, lifted me slightly up off my heels and planted the most passionate kiss on my lips. We sat there kissing for the longest time, and then he sweetly and gently lowered me back down and led me over to his sofa.

We both sat down and looked at each other. I finally spoke and said, "Wow! I don't think I can do that at the office."

He reached across and brushed a hair off my cheek. "I know," he said and shifted to adjust himself. "But it felt damned great!"

"What's the deal with Monica?" I asked.

Kale frowned and replied, "She wanted some strange revision to the script."

"What?" I asked.

"She wanted to rewrite the heroine so that she commits suicide," he said. "I told her it wasn't a black comedy. She insisted and then got really mad."

I sighed and decided to muster up the steam to ask the forbidden question because, with all of the displays of affection, I figured maybe it was time. "Are you fucking Monica?"

Kale pulled away and was clearly taken aback by that question. "I don't fuck my staff," he said and seemed offended.

"I'm sorry," I replied and felt bad for assuming. "I just

— noticed something there."

Kale grabbed me by my lower back and slid me across the sofa so he could kiss me again. "Sweetheart, you're imagining it."

We kissed for a few minutes more, and then I pulled completely back. "I can't do this. I just want to make love, and we're not doing that yet," I said and got up.

Kale smiled and nodded. "Of course."

I started to leave and then turned back to him. "Just for the record, we're both dating other people, right?"

Kale stood up, nodded and smiled: "I know you'll be mine."

He returned to his desk, smiled sweetly at me and then went back to his iPad. I returned his smile and headed out the door. Just as I exited, my iPhone chirped with a text message. I looked down and was surprised to see a message from Johnny. I hadn't heard from him in days. He asked me to lunch, to which I readily agreed. We were friends after all. Just as I was typing on my keyboard, I smacked right into Curtis. Startled, I looked up and stepped away, but Curtis stepped to the same side. He looked around. No one was in view, and he attempted to lean down to kiss me to which I responded by jerking backward and nearly falling over.

"What the hell are you doing?" I snapped.

Curtis reached out to grab my breast, and once again, I jerked even further back. His expression wasn't open and friendly, but dark and stern. "Did you fuck Kale?" he asked in a low-baritone voice.

I just stared at him, determined not to answer his question.

"Fuck off," I snapped again and turned quickly to maneuver away. I heard him start laughing in this threatening, alarming tone. Curtis had been creepy, and now he was just scary. I didn't know if it was time to tell Kale or not. They appeared to be friends, but Curtis was starting to frighten me. I sighed and considered my options. What would I tell Kale without starting some kind of office war? I couldn't think of a single thing that wouldn't turn out badly. "Shit!" I muttered to myself.

I got to my office to find a gold box that looked like it contained flowers had been delivered and left on my desk. I smiled and thought of Kale. I lifted the box to read the card taped to the big, black ribbon. The black ribbon seemed rather odd. Why would a florist tie a black ribbon to the box? I opened the card, but it was blank. How strange. I then opened the box only to find a dozen dead red roses. I was stunned and stepped back from it. Who the hell would send me dead roses? I stood there and stared at them completely upset. Was it Curtis? But to do that in front of everyone would be ballsy and bring accusations out in the open. I didn't think Curtis would be that stupid.

Just then, Erin walked in and stared, too. "Oh!" she cried. "Who sent those?"

I shook my head and my eyes watered. Erin came over and hugged me. "Should we tell Kale?" she asked.

We didn't have to. Kale had come down the hallway and must have heard Erin's cry. He stepped in and stared at the strange box loaded with dead plant material. He looked stunned. I just stood next to Erin and didn't say a word.

"Sweetheart, what the hell?" he asked, very upset by the

delivery. "Who sent those?"

I shook my head. Erin stepped away, and Kale moved close to me in a protective way. He grabbed the box off the desk. "Fuck this!" he said and stalked out of the room to discard the ugliness. He soon returned and whispered something to Erin, which prompted her to leave. He grabbed me and hugged me very close.

"Are you okay?" he asked.

I nodded and looked down. I felt ashamed. I had upset someone enough that he went this far to send me dead flowers. I don't know why, but all this guilt and humiliation washed over me like a black ugliness that made me want to recoil from Kale. Kale must have sensed the tension in my body.

He gazed at me with such concern and said, "Now what's this about?"

I continued to feel badly about myself. I just shook my head and swiped away a tear.

"Come on, Brea," he cajoled. "Don't go there." He then shifted a bit and kind of looked at me strangely. "Unless, you're hiding something again?"

There! There it was! The reason we weren't back together. He just said the underlying problem. I felt everything from hurt to pain to guilt and shame. And then worse, a surge of anger now directed at my former lover. He must have seen the emotions cycle. He suddenly grabbed me and yanked me so close I could barely breathe. What was going on? I wanted to cry, but then again, I felt too much shock and numbness to let go. I wrapped my arms around Kale and held on. I then slowly tilted my face toward his lips. We began to kiss with a tender fragility. I wanted to relent, give in and just make love, but we were close but also so far apart from each other; we had fallen into this strange emotional gap.

Kale pulled away and said, "Do you want to talk?"

"No," I replied. "I need to work."

He just stared at me for a moment more, and then reluctantly left my side. I could tell he didn't want to go. I just wanted to be alone. I didn't know which way was up or down right then. I was afraid of Curtis. I just received dead roses, and Kale had up-ended our relationship with a quiet, unspoken and forbidden accusation. Something split, cracked and broke inside of me – something deep and painful. I didn't know, in that moment, if it were even possible for Kale and I to really find our way back to each other. And I knew what was true about what I had done in those last six months. Consequences. We make choices – and every choice has its consequence. Kale's mistrust and the dark accusation were the fallout from my weakness and poor judgment. Would this trouble and mistrust ever go away, or would it sit between us forever like decaying rot that eats at a relationship?

Chapter 15

I don't know if Johnny just wanted to mess with me, but he had me meet him at Johnny Rockets restaurant, which had a festive drive-in, diner-like atmosphere and served pretty good burgers. Any good California girl knows that hamburgers will make you fat – that and greasy French fries, which Johnny Rockets served plenty of in red baskets. We ended up sitting on the patio at a small table for two, and I did order a burger, fries and a Diet Coke. It sounded good, and I was starving since I rarely ate breakfast and drank coffee and cream almost every morning just to start my engine.

When I walked up, Johnny could tell something was amiss. I shrugged it off as a work problem. He immediately quizzed me about when I thought they would start production since he had won the lead role of my former lover and nemesis Drew. He kept digging about Drew, too, and asking me what he was like and about his mannerisms. He wanted to really capture the "essence" of the real Drew, which was slightly disturbing to me. I pointed out that the character was loosely based on the real Drew – and that it was a comedy anyway. What Drew had done to me with his seduction and giving me the drug Ecstasy to secure his place in my bed didn't seem remotely funny. It had certainly destroyed my relationship with Kale, and the cost just seemed to add up that very day.

Johnny then told me that he and Ryan had had an argument. Something about Johnny going for a part at Ryan's dad's production studio, and Ryan not being supportive. I tried to understand what Ryan did or what would motivate him to hurt his friend's chances at a movie role, but Johnny was vague. He just ranted that Ryan was a user and an asshole. He had kicked Johnny out, and Johnny didn't understand why.

Then he cocked his head at me, smiled and asked, "Are you still hanging out with him?"

"Sort of," I replied, picking up a fry and stuffing it into my mouth.

"He's a user," he reiterated. "Don't get sucked in, Brea. He likes to fuck with girls' heads. Hangs out with them. He never commits. He's a total 'phobe' about it. You're a nice girl. Stay away from him."

I got real curious and asked, "You don't think he would do something weird like send someone dead flowers?"

Johnny fidgeted, looked at me strangely and then shook his head. "Nah, he's not a stalker."

I felt infinitely better about that answer. We soon exited Johnny Rockets and went out to my car. I stood next to my Corolla to say good-bye when Johnny leaned in to kiss me. I pulled away and shook my head. "I don't like this – and you're in the movie. Plus, you handed me to your former friend."

"My mistake," he chuckled and moved forward just a bit so I was backed against the car. He then leaned in and whispered, "I want to have sex."

I shook my head. God! What was it about this day? And I had had enough of the come-ons already. "No, it's a bad idea. But look, it was good to see you."

Johnny looked slightly disappointed and said, "You're not saving it for Ryan, are you?"

"Johnny, enough!" I retorted and felt frustrated by all of these guys and the sex thing. I felt like Johnny's ping-pong ball, what with him passing me off to Ryan in the first place. "I'm leaving," I said in a flat tone before turning and getting into my car.

Johnny relented and left. I sat in my hot car for a moment and looked down at my phone. A text message from Lance had come in. He was hospitalized. Shit! He must have gotten sicker. I decided to drive straight over to Cedars-Sinai and see him.

I soon arrived at the hospital and walked straight into the lobby. The cool air rushed at me like a brisk breeze, and I could immediately smell that faint sterile odor of a hospital – a smell that always unsettled me. Like most people, I was not a fan of hospitals. The lobby area was clean with industrial blue carpet and lounge chairs positioned on each side of the entryway. The information desk sat below a large, round sunroof with a dangling mobile strung from the middle that hung like a chandelier and shimmered like ivory in the bright daylight. I asked for Lance's room and got directed to the furthest wing on the upper floor.

As I dashed off the elevator, the unpleasant smell of hospital food and warmed-over death seemed to come out at me. I hated that smell. It was a cross between something rotting and Lysol. I found Lance's room number and peered in. I could see his thinned frame hidden beneath a powder-blue blanket and a red dew rag covering his baldness. He stirred and twisted to see me. He smiled, but I could tell he was too weak to sit up. Tubes ran from one arm – one feeding him intravenously and another delivering medicine from bags strung up on steel hooks. Lance's face was pale, but sweet with his hopeful smile. I walked over, leaned over him and he jerked forward to catch my lips on his own. I kissed him with affection. He moved over just enough and welcomed me into his bed. I granted his wish and slid right in. He wrapped his thin arm around my shoulders and pulled me to his chest. We lay like lovers, only we were no longer – and it was okay with both of us.

I saw a woman who I assumed was his mother, an older woman who looked to be in her fifties, come to the door, stop and then graciously disappear to give us space. I surmised Lance had told her I was coming and had asked for privacy. I couldn't imagine what he told her about me. Did he describe us as former lovers? Did he admit he wasn't over me? Did he even hope for us to be together anymore? I knew that if he were well, he would have been trying to make love to me, but in this condition the best he could do was hold me like a lover would. I deeply and truly cared about him. He was my friend and rock. The one thing about Lance was I could always depend on him for reassurance and understanding. Now I wanted to give him the same comfort he had always shown me in my moments of darkness.

I suddenly raised my hand and looked at him. "Are you dying?" I heard myself ask in the most surreal, out-of-body way.

"Pneumonia," he said quietly and coughed a bit when he managed to speak. "I could die, but we all die," he said as he tried to take in more air and coughed again.

"Don't talk," I said quietly.

"God, I would love to fuck you right now," he said with a laugh and coughed again.

"The last supper?" I laughed. "One last great orgasm. If you want … "

Lance leaned down a bit and kissed my forehead. I ran my head on his bulge beneath the blanket, but nothing stirred. He chuckled at the gesture. I just stroked him anyway because I knew it still felt good. After a moment, he grabbed my hand and moved it up to his chest. I could feel his breath was labored. I felt tears well up in my eyes and slide gently down my cheeks. I didn't look up. I didn't want him to see me cry. As the afternoon wore on and we lay quietly together, Lance fell into a deep sleep. I could hear his breath steadily rising and falling. I looked up into his placid, white complexion. He really looked peaceful. I had wanted his advice about Curtis and the flowers, but then again, he would worry and stress over it. I didn't want that for him right now. When I knew he was out for the evening, I slid carefully out of the bed. I went to the door to leave, turned and looked at him. He was sleeping deeply and looked serene. I slipped quietly out of his room and left.

When I pulled up to my apartment complex some time later, Ryan was there. He had arrived earlier, and I walked in the room to find him thumb-wrestling Denise. They were laughing like two little pranksters, and their dark tennis shoes were locked together as they tried to knock the other off balance. Ryan had this vibrant and fun energy about him all of the time, and he was just laughing with pure joy at the game. When I came in, he looked at me with such an infectious, happy grin. Denise was giggling and finally her thumb overcame his, and she raised her arms up like an Olympic athlete to declare herself the thumb-wrestling champion of the world. Ryan was more than happy to let her grab that title. He came over to me and lightly kissed my lips to greet me.

"Hey, babe," he said. "I've got plans for us."

"Plans? Uh — I don't know."

Denise stood in the hallway entryway and leaned against the doorframe. She looked at me quizzically and tilted her head in a sort of strange and questioning way. She grabbed a red Tootsie Pop, unwrapped it and plunged it in her mouth. Now she watched us like a spectator at a football game as she sucked the lollipop. I looked over at her and wondered what this look was all about.

"Your friend Curtis called," she offered.

"He's not my friend," I barked back.

"Well, he said he wants to send you some paperwork. You're

not signing with him, are you?" she asked with concern.

I was alarmed and replied, "No!"

"So come on," Ryan bellowed and headed for the door. "We've got things to do. Places to conquer," he cried and laughed as he walked out the door.

He had assumed I would follow, and you know what? I did. Ryan had impeccable timing. Every time shitty stuff seemed to happen, here was Mr. Happy-Go-Lucky ready to distract my cares away. As soon as the door closed behind us, I jumped on his back, and we trotted out to his black Range Rover. He set me down on the ground in front of the passenger's side door and turned around. I jumped up and wrapped my legs around his waist to kiss him with fervor. He pulled away with such a fun smile on his face.

"I had a shitty, shitty day," I offered.

Ryan nodded and kissed me passionately again. "We'll take care of that later!" he promised and opened the car door for me to get in. "But first … " his voice trailed off.

I had my own raging desire going on. A lot of sexual frustration was building up, but I also wanted an adventure, and Ryan was always the man for fun. So, he got in, and we soon pulled away from the curb and were off to places unknown.

As we were driving, I got curious and wanted to know why he and Johnny were no longer talking or even friends. I was leaning on the armrest toward him and decided to find out. I was slightly disturbed, after all, about Johnny's warning and didn't want to play completely dumb. But I didn't intend for this fling with Ryan to be anything more serious, and I didn't want him to think that was my intention either. All the while, Ryan was talking about going to Australia for the winter to catch some "wicked" waves and get away from LA, the "smog pit" of California. I couldn't exactly disagree about the smog part – it was perpetually smoggy and that haze settled over the basin pretty regularly.

"You ought to meet my dad," he suddenly offered and changed the subject away from surfing in Australia. "Man, you should sell him your next script. He'll probably pay you bank if I hit him up!" he said with a charming laugh.

I shrugged and said, "Maybe."

My mind drifted with the idea for a moment. I did want to develop my career past my relationship with Kale. The idea of being dependent on him for my next project didn't sound like a good one. The fragility of our relationship might destroy that opportunity at some point, and then I had to deal with the impending shadow of Curtis, who I still thought might have sent those dead flowers. Should I tell Ryan about the flowers? I quickly decided not to. Ryan was too caught up in his own fun-fueled world filled with parties, endless days at the beach, rock climbing, skydiving and an assortment of other "wicked" activities that kept him from having any true meaning in his life. What was so likeable about Ryan, though, was that he was absolutely the real deal – a playboy seemingly without a care in the world who didn't worry about his lack of ambition.

"So, I saw Johnny," I said and managed to bring up the forbidden topic that Ryan so artfully avoided.

"Fuck him," said Ryan as his demeanor shifted away from

his perpetual smile and gleam in his eyes.

"What happened?" I asked.

Ryan shifted and got really uncomfortable. "Babe, let's not talk about Johnny."

I looked down and didn't want to pry. It seemed Ryan wasn't going to tell me anyway and pushy wasn't really my style on personal matters. I noticed we had pulled into a big complex of industrial-type buildings. The sign out front read: "Boing-O." I saw a bunch of mostly guys heading for the entrance. Ryan parked, got out, opened the back of the Range Rover and came round. He opened my door and tossed tennis shoes and socks into my lap.

"What is this place?" I asked, looking down at my Nikes and white socks.

"Trampoline land, babe," he said with a broad smile. "It's awesome."

I was wearing walking shorts and a pink tank top so at least I didn't need to change. I tossed off my black flip-flops and put on the socks and tennis shoes. I wasn't totally sure what we were going to be doing, but I was game. Ryan led the way as we walked into a concrete stadium complex that had three levels of wall-to-wall trampolines with padding on the edges to protect participants. I just stared at the people bouncing on the trampolines, performing flips, tucks and rolls. I couldn't help it and just let out a laugh. I hadn't been on a trampoline since I was in the fifth grade. I was gawking at the bouncers when I felt Ryan grab me by the arm and pull me forward toward one of the huge bounce areas.

We got to the entrance, and he grabbed my wrist and tied a yellow bracelet around it to clear entry – and then like a mad bunny he sprang off literally tumbling first and then bouncing and flipping and there he did it. He jumped high and flip-flopped from one trampoline to another with the grace of a professional gymnast. I was literally standing there, staring in surprise, and bouncing up and down as all around me people were stepping on and off the trampolines.

Ryan landed clear on the other side of the open space, and he gave me a boisterous wave to join him. I looked around and watched the other people effortlessly bounce from one trampoline to another. I looked down and around and started to bounce and pick up speed, and when I had worked up enough steam, I propelled myself forward toward him. I bounced high, screeched with the thrill of it and bounced to him like a little kid in a bouncy house. I used my arms to thrust forward, and soon I landed in front of him. He grabbed both arms, and we bounced together and started picking up momentum so we were bouncing super high. As he landed first, his weight caused tension that made me spring up like a rocket even higher than him. My arms swung around to try and steady myself – and I was laughing so uncontrollably by this time. I felt like a little girl and just went with the fun. We hopped, sprang and bounced all over the place. Ryan was laughing just as uproariously, only he knew how to flip and fly in synch with his perpetual laughter. I watched his muscles tense and release – what a cut body he had. He was quite a sight.

We bounced for two hours (the limit of our passes) and

filed out back to the parking lot – both of us fueled on adrenaline and the joy of living. When we got back to the Range Rover, Ryan leaned against it with his legs slightly apart and welcomed me into him. I walked right up to him and we fell into a passionate, playful kiss.

He looked down at me with such a smirk and said, "You want to go fuck like rabbits?"

I nodded, and he opened the car to let me climb in the passenger side. He drove back to his house and when he opened the door, he walked out ahead of me and began stripping off his clothes to leave a trail all the way out to the back patio and the Jacuzzi tub next to the pool. He climbed right in, then just sat there and waited for me. The steam rose up above his head, and he spread his arms out along the edge with an infectious grin on his face. This guy was just like an upper of fun and mischief. I liked him.

I stripped and left my own trail of clothes. I stopped at the edge of the Jacuzzi so Ryan could measure my naked body with his eyes. He continued to grin like a self-satisfied prince. I walked slowly along the edge of the Jacuzzi to allow his eyes to freely wander over my body. He kept the same grin on his face, and as I slowly stepped down into the water, he moved smoothly across and pulled me with both hands around my waist onto his lap. We began to kiss passionately. He positioned himself just so and helped me slide onto him. As he penetrated, I gasped a little in excitement. He grabbed me by the face and leveled his gaze into my eyes.

"Fuck me hard," he growled like a hungry animal.

I kept my eyes fixed on his and began rocking up and down on him. He broke his gaze and ran his wet mouth down my neck to my breasts where he used his tongue very gently on my nipple before he tenderly bit down slightly. It sent a surge through me, and I gasped and sucked in air. I rocked harder and pressed forward into him so I could pleasure myself. The pleasure was building up, and I had felt so frustrated with the unreleased desire of the past few days that I effortlessly let go and an orgasm rippled and quivered through my thighs. I cried out in delight, which in turn, made Ryan come back up to my mouth to kiss me hard as he picked up speed and grunted in lust and enjoyment.

"I'm going to cum," he breathlessly declared as he raised my hips up and down with a rapid rocking. He suddenly pulled me up, flipped me over and started fucking me doggy style against the edge of the Jacuzzi. I held onto the edge as my multiple orgasms continued to flutter through my body. He began to rapidly pound me, and I screamed a little, which in turn, excited him, and he, too, released and came hard. He again made a low growl and moan, bent over me for a moment to stroke my breasts from behind, and then stood up, slapped my ass and pulled back.

"Yeah!" he declared as he sat back against the bench of the Jacuzzi. "Girl, you're fine!"

I got my bearings back and moved over to his lap, where he warmly accepted me and wrapped his arms all the way around my body so I was gripped in a bear hug. He kissed the back of my neck.

"Damn girl! I might have to give up my Wednesday fuck for you," he offered as if this were some loving gesture.

I turned, splashed him a little and said, "Oh, don't give up anything for me."

He buried his face in the nape of my neck and purred, "But you're so *goood.*"

I turned over and straddled him so we faced each other. I looked him straight in the eyes. "Just keep me as your fuck buddy, all right?"

Ryan just grandly smiled and replied, "Yes, ma'am. As long as you fuck me one more time tonight."

I softened a bit, kissed him and replied, "Absolutely." And we did it three more times.

Chapter 16

Production on my movie officially began after a scheduling conflict with two of the actors was resolved. Kale decided to roll cameras early to meet all of the different scheduling demands. A great deal of primary photography was going to be done in and around LA, which made it pretty convenient for me. I thought Kale might choose to film in locations outside of town – and some listed on the run sheet were in neighboring communities – but for the most part it would be shot in town.

The first day of shooting, I didn't know what I was feeling exactly. I thought I should be more excited, but that morning a series of blocked calls came to my cell number followed by hang-ups. I was getting disturbed about the calls and dead flowers, but then decided not to let this screw up my first day on a film set, which was a brand new experience.

I drove up to a parking lot outside of Santa Monica where they had mocked up a bikini shop in an abandoned boutique, which, because of the recession, was still vacant. I told Letty all about how her shop would become infamous. Being Letty, she only laughed and begged to be an extra. When I asked Kale, he said fine and so she would be off and on set, which made me happy to have a friend to hang around with. I wasn't sure how much rewriting would be required since this was the first film I had written and produced. I just went to the set with my MacBook Air tucked in my bag. When I pulled up, I noticed vans lined up against the street's edge. Kale had instructed me to park and then take a van to the set because the roads outside would be blocked off.

I got out of the car and walked over to a van sitting there solo with a driver waiting and talking on his cell. When I got into the van, I broadly and proudly smiled and declared I was the writer. The sweet, fat gentleman who looked Indian just grinned at me with a semi-toothless smile. Just as he was about to pull out, I heard someone call out – it was Maya. She breathlessly yanked open the van's sliding door and gave me the wildest scream of excitement.

"Chica!" she declared, leaping in and hugging me with such enthusiasm. "You excited, sí?"

"I guess," I said. "It's kind of surreal, though."

"Ah, you get used to it," she replied. "My chica going to be muy famous!"

"I think that's reserved for the actors," I replied.

"Sí, but the actors no look like you – bonita!"

The van pulled away from the curb and drove down to the pier, bumping over gutters and potholes. The loose springs in the bench seat made us bounce up and down like little school children. Maya only giggled with each jolt. I became more and more introverted as we pulled up and saw the masses of trucks, trailers and generators lined along the street. I felt completely outside of myself; these people were all here because of a story I had imagined in my head. To think that without my imagination, none of these people would be here on this set doing their jobs. I think that freaked me out just a little.

We got out of the van and my eyes scanned for Kale, who was standing with several people around him. I hung back for a moment to let him work without interruption. I noticed Curtis was standing very tight with him, smiling and talking in a low voice. I kept wondering what he was saying. Monica was sitting quietly under a tent off to one side, and she looked serious and pensive. She never said much directly to me anyway.

A cute dark-haired production assistant rushed up and offered coffee, to which I said "yes," and Maya declined. Kale was reading a clipboard and looking down, but he finally glanced up and saw me. His eyes met mine – and he quickly handed the board to Curtis, who turned and saw me too. I couldn't tell what the look on Curtis' face meant. Did he look annoyed, angry or conniving? I couldn't tell, and I had a quick thought that I felt relieved I had not confessed the Curtis problem to Kale. It seemed inevitable it would have tainted this important day.

Kale walked straight over to us and positioned himself in the middle so he could hug us both with the same affection. "Ladies," he said with such a sweet smile of pleasure. "So, sweetheart, what do you think?"

I really didn't know what I thought exactly. It was too weird for words to describe how I felt. I noticed two crewmembers carrying a sign with a logo and the bikini shop name. I felt nauseous as a spark of nerves electrified my body. I wanted to run and vomit in the nearest garbage can. Kale must have noticed my complexion turn a slight shade of green, and he became serious. He withdrew from Maya so he could quietly talk me out of my self-made tree of anxiety.

He leaned over like a gentle giant with a child and looked me right in the eyes. "You okay, sweetheart?" he asked with concern. "Do you need something? Water?"

I shook my head and tried to shake off the building panic attack. Kale, my sweet man, pulled me closer and pushed the hair off my face. "Tell me, what's wrong?"

"I don't know – it's just … weird" was the only explanation I could offer him.

Kale laughed with amusement. He smiled like a devil at me, pulled me into a hug and whispered into my ear, "I would rather take you on a long boat ride where we could make love all day."

I looked at him – and he was completely sincere. He brushed a light kiss on my lips and added in a soft voice, "When will you say you love me?"

I felt my eyes water up. Kale yanked me even closer and held me tenderly for a moment. "Don't cry," he soothed. He pulled away. "Now let's make a movie."

The production assistant showed up with coffee and interrupted right in time. The associate director, some guy named Paul, came over to speak with Kale. Kale directed me to his trailer to wait while he went off to talk to Paul. I took my coffee and walked over to the trailer with Maya right behind me. Maya had been engaged in what looked like a flirtation with the grip girl, but when I walked off toward the trailer she ran after me to catch up. I walked up the step, pulled the latch on the trailer door and opened it. I stepped in to find it was decorated like an upscale living room with a huge, black flat-screen TV against the front wall, two brown velour sofas on each side, a full kitchen and dining area toward the back, and a door open to reveal a bedroom at the very back. I was astonished, but somehow not surprised.

I moved to the dining area to sit and drink my coffee in peace. Maya followed me and sat in the U-shaped booth slightly across from me. "What's going on with Kale?" she asked.

"Nothing," I replied quietly.

"I know he loves you," she said with confidence. Then she became antsy, got up and went to the sink. Maya was going to clean the trailer. I almost laughed aloud, but refrained.

"He doesn't trust me," I admitted.

Just then the trailer door swung open and in came Johnny and Ryan. Now I was confused. What happened to their fighting? Maya turned and looked at them in amazement.

"I have to go to makeup," said Johnny. "Ryan wanted to see you."

And with that announcement, Johnny disappeared right back out the door. Ryan jumped like some crazy Tigger into the booth, which made the whole trailer bounce. He kissed me passionately right on the lips, which I allowed but felt uncomfortable about with Maya in the room and her feelings about the situation. I was sure Kale wouldn't appreciate the sudden appearance of my overly energized lover. Maya looked right at

Ryan with a shocked expression.

"Who you?" she cried, her Spanish accent thickening as it always did when she was emotional.

"Who me?" Ryan replied with such an effervescent, enthused smile it was hard to be mad at him.

"Maya, this is Ryan," I introduced them.

Maya seemed less than satisfied with that response. She steamed up and got very angry. "And you wonder why he no trust you," she cried, grabbed her purse where she had left it on the sofa and marched out.

Ryan's mouth dropped open and then he threw his head back with a wonderfully robust laugh. "Babe, why would anyone trust you? You're too hot to settle for one guy."

I turned to Ryan and stared. "Hey!" I shouted. "I can be a one-guy girl."

Ryan scooted closer. "Really?"

I stared at him and then looked away. I didn't want to answer that question. Ryan was fidgeting and hyper. He reached under the table to run his hand up my leg toward my bush. I gasped for a moment and then reached down and knocked his hand away. "I'm working."

"So am I," he said with just a wide smile. Then he moved closer and kissed me. "There's a bed back there," he said.

"Ryan, no!" I refused him. I couldn't do that in Kale's trailer. It was tacky and inappropriate.

Ryan shrugged and bounced out of the booth. He was completely unfazed and totally gregarious. "I'm going surfing," he said. "Wish you were here!" he said that phrase like it was a greeting card slogan, and then he bound out of the trailer like the same old crazy Tigger.

I sat there completely amazed and realized I hadn't had time to ask him about Johnny. I figured I would ask Johnny about it later. The door opened again only this time it was Monica. She stared at me and came over. I said hi, but she barely said anything back. She handed me a current script, half-smiled and went to leave.

She stopped abruptly at the door. "Was that your boyfriend?"

"Not really," I said.

"Oh," she said. "He's cute."

"He's totally cute," I replied, frowned and wondered what was her point.

"Does Kale know him?" she asked.

Now she was annoying me. What was with the personal questions? "Sort of," I responded.

"Oh," she said and left.

I shook my head and opened the script she had given me. It was littered with different colored pages to indicate changes to the original script. It looked like a rainbow. I just smiled. Such was my life as a screenwriter – and it felt damned great to be one.

Chapter 17

After a long 14-hour day on the set, Kale finally returned to his trailer alone. I had retired to the plushy bed with the huge light-blue comforter on top. Kale walked into the small bedroom, and with each step the trailer shook under his weight. The shaking was what woke me up. I had just dozed off. Kale slid across the bed to rest beside me. He sighed, gently grabbed me and pulled me to his chest where I rested my head.

"First day of shooting is always long," he offered in a quiet voice.

"Uh-huh," I responded with my eyes closed. "I love your bed," I added.

"I love you in my bed," he said, and I could hear the pleasure in his voice.

"I didn't think you would mind," I replied.

"That Ry-Ry guy stopped in," he said. "What did he want?"

"For me to go surfing," I answered.

"Surfing? Do you surf, sweetheart?"

"No, but maybe I'll learn," I responded as I moved up and kissed his pink lips. He felt warm and a little sweaty. I wanted him as usual. I wondered how long we were going to be able to keep this dance up. He had been so restrained when I knew he wasn't the kind of guy to normally keep his urges under such close control. I pulled away, opened my tired eyes and met his gaze. I wanted to tell him what he wanted to hear. I did love him, but he didn't want to just be lovers, and I wasn't ready for more. I just felt too young to tie myself down in a relationship I really believed could be special and quite serious. I didn't want him to feel rejected either – every fiber in my body wanted him. I felt comfortable and at ease. We fit together so wholly – and every time I thought we were okay and healing, the mention of trust would arise like some unwanted party crasher.

"We can learn together – I've always wanted to surf," he said and leaned down and pulled my full body to rest on top of his much longer torso. The minute he did so, I felt him become immediately aroused and hard. This temptation was just a little too much for me. I kissed him, and he grabbed me by the back of the neck and kissed me with such lust and passion. I felt his tongue probe my mouth and taste me. I pulled gently back, slid carefully off him and sat on the edge of the bed.

"Do you trust me?" I asked bluntly.

I heard Kale sigh. He moved up and sat back against the headboard. I felt like I could hear his thoughts firing like pistons in his mind. He was quiet long enough to suggest he was weighing out a thoughtful response. "Are we back here again?" he asked so quietly it was barely audible. I heard regret in his voice and pain.

I turned and looked right at him. “I’m sorry for that,” I said. “It’s my fault. But the real question is will it ever change? Even if I told you I loved you, it doesn’t matter if you don’t trust me.”

Kale slid over to me and swung his long legs over the edge of the bed so that we were now sitting side by side. He wrapped his muscular arm around my shoulders and leaned all the way over so he could catch my eyes. “I want it, too, sweetheart,” he said with such a kind smile of reassurance.

I sighed, sucked in air and then released it as I said, “All right. So two hurdles.”

I crawled right up onto his lap and planted a passionate kiss on his lips. I pulled away, and we both smiled right at each other. I jumped off and up, grabbed my bag and stood there for a moment. “If I stay, I won’t be able to keep holding back.”

“Goodnight.” He blinked and nodded.

I smiled and headed out toward the door. Goodnight for now, I thought.

Chapter 18

As I exited the trailer, Letty and Ryan showed up together. It hit me what a crazy couple the two of them would make: Letty with her strange mercurial style and Ryan with his endless, crazy energy and enthusiasm would certainly be able to share wild stories. Ryan's hair was tousled and a little dingy from the sand and surf. His cheeks were bright pink from too much sun, and he gleamed with radiance and energy, which he always did. Upon questioning about how they came in contact, Ryan said he had been a frequent visitor of the surf shop that Letty also managed, and that he had spotted her on set only to discover their mutual friendship with me. Johnny came up to our gathering fresh from his last scene, and his face was still damp from removing the makeup.

"Y'all want to go clubbing?" he asked with a huge and inviting smile.

Just as he asked, Kale stepped out of the trailer door right behind us. I turned and looked over my shoulder at my tall man, who looked somewhat taken aback by this scene. He had overheard Johnny's question – I could tell by the look on his face. When Kale appeared silence fell over our group.

We all acted like our father had walked in the room – a bunch of guilty teenagers. While Kale wasn't that much older than us, he had this gravitas to his very presence. It also didn't exactly help that both Letty and Ryan had untamed energy about them. I would not call Ryan immature, but he was a free spirit and quite the opposite of Kale, who, even with family money, had built his business on his own. Both of these qualities made each man simply appealing and adorable to me for different reasons.

"Y'all going out?" asked Kale with a slight mocking tone. He stared right at Ryan as if his glare would somehow scare him away from me. Kale stepped forward and wrapped his arm around me in more of a protective way than just being territorial. I could tell he simply didn't like Ryan, and I was aware that perhaps he was no fan of Johnny's either.

Anxiety crossed Johnny's face, which was understandable since Kale was his boss. Ryan, though, looked defiant, and I could see he didn't much care for Kale's arm around me either. I had mentioned to Ryan that I saw Kale regularly, but that we were not sleeping together. Ryan, being the happy charmer, didn't seem fazed by this admission until the reality was right in front of him. Ryan had no right to get territorial. We had zero commitment or even the question or promise there ever would be one. While Ryan may or may not have cut down on his many female relationships, I had never asked him to. The menagerie of men all in one place was awkward and uncomfortable. I quickly slid out from under Kale's arm, looked at everyone and just laughed.

"Why are you laughing?" Ryan asked and frowned. His happy face had morphed into dismay and maybe a hint of anger.

"Come on!" I waved. "Let's all go out!" I suggested and moved toward the parked vans where the last of the drivers were waiting to take people back to their cars.

Kale and Ryan sized each other up, and it was Ryan whose frown dissipated into a strange glee. Of all people, Ryan got it. Well, Ryan got me. He started laughing and trailed right behind me. Letty and Johnny soon followed, and it was Kale, my reluctant friend and former lover, who finally relented and came along. Only he rushed up to join me. We all piled into the vans, and all the tension drifted away into Letty telling dirty jokes and gossiping about the other extras. Johnny was a bit more guarded with his boss around, but he did share some humorous moments about how his costar, an up-and-coming actress, botched her lines fives times.

When I got to my car, I stopped in my tracks. Kale came to stand beside me. Under my windshield wiper, another dead rose had been shoved and left for me to find. The others had piled into Ryan's Range Rover up the street, so they were not with me for this latest discovery. Underneath the rose was a yellow sticky note. Kale stepped forward, grabbed the rose and threw it away, and looked at the sticky note, which read in big red letters: "BITCH!"

Now I was frightened. Someone knew I was here. He was continuing with the dead roses and writing nasty notes. What had I done to provoke anyone? I knew I wasn't perfect, but the only person I had really hurt was standing next to me and pulling me into him. Kale was deeply concerned and looked at me.

"Maybe we ought to report this?" he offered with worry on his face. "It's the second time, and whoever it is seems to know where to find you."

I was silent for a moment and considered the offer. He was right. We should report it. And then there was the phone calls – he didn't know about those hang-ups, which I quickly told him about. He became even more concerned. He grabbed his iPhone and called the local police. He was routed through the system and finally spoke to an officer, who advised me to come in to file the report about the harassment so that, if at some point I figured out who was doing it, I could file a restraining order. After finishing the phone conversation, Kale offered to follow me back to my house. I figured the others would be fine without me.

When I got to my apartment, Kale stepped out of his car and walked over to mine and opened my car for me – ever the gentlemen. He walked me upstairs and then we stood in front of the door for a moment. I opened up and invited him in. He looked around my small, but sweet space.

"You've never invited me in your home before," he said with such a Kale-like smile of pleasure. "It's charming, sweetheart."

"Thanks," I replied and looked straight up into his translucent blue-green eyes. I was tired and wanted him to hold me close. He seemed to read my mind and grabbed me by the back of the neck and gently pulled me into his chest. He wrapped his long, lean arms all the way around me in a full hug and held me closely and lovingly for a good five minutes. His affection and warmth soothed away the anxiety.

He finally pulled away, kissed me ever so gently and said, "I have an early call. I shouldn't have agreed to go out, but I so enjoyed the look on Ry-Ry's face. I think he has stronger feelings for you, Brea, than you think. Maybe you ought to quit fucking him."

I looked up at him and nodded. "I am apparently a heartless bitch. Maybe I ought to move to Tibet and live in a monastery," I sarcastically replied. "Think the dead-rose asshole would stop harassing me then?"

"Why do you suppose it's a guy, sweetheart?" Kale asked what I quickly realized was a good question. Yes, why did I assume that? I didn't know who it was. I guess I had figured it was Curtis, but what did I know? It could be anyone – male or female. It crossed my mind that maybe it was Drew. Drew was crazy enough to harass me. He had done so many inappropriate things in the past, what would stop him from doing this? I quickly decided I would pay him a little visit in the morning.

"Good point," I replied and stepped forward. I tilted my head up, grabbed Kale by the back of the neck and pulled him into a long, passionate kiss. Kale made a quiet "hmm" noise – he was enjoying this kiss. He lingered in it and then very slowly his tongue sensually probed my mouth. That was it! I couldn't do this anymore. I pushed him away.

"All right, I'm just going to tell you," I said with the sheer force of will to be honest. "I think you're the one. I'm only 22, Kale! Twenty-two! I don't know if I'm even old enough to know if I should say to anyone, 'You're the one.' I have big, big lust for you. I want you all of the time. I wish I hadn't fucked us up, but then again, that's part of the problem – I'm 22!" I said this in a high-pitched, anxious voice. "You're what, 30 or 32? You've lived this whole other life without me. You've made it. You have stories and experiences. Me? None of that! I'm not ready for any of this, and deep down maybe that's why I did what I did."

"Thirty-five," Kale offered his age, which was really funny and made me laugh a little. I couldn't even judge his age correctly. And I'm not sure that admission made it any better, but it made it make more sense. He was ready for all the things these intense feelings we shared brought to life. I was 13 years younger. Why I had never wondered his exact age until now, I was surprised. I also felt so stupid, I could easily have made myself the brunt of a good joke about dumb blondes.

"Okay then ... 35, and now you get my point!" I replied. "I have years of catching up to do. And I'm a royal fuckup, okay! I fucked another man during our relationship." The minute the confession came out of my mouth was the very same moment I realized I had never told Kale that information. The look on Kale's face could have sliced me open. He literally took that admission like a blow to the gut and reeled backward toward the door. His eyes widened. His clear eyes were open and hurt – I had done it. I had wielded the last painful knife in our already shaky relationship. He clearly had been under the assumption it was just the kiss he had witnessed that day in Teenie's Bikinis. He didn't know about the infidelity. The truth seared a hole into his heart. He didn't even say anything to me. He just stood there and stared into me like he truly could not speak.

"Oh god, Kale! Shit!" I cried and tried to approach him, but he only stepped away from me in revulsion.

Kale's mouth was open. "I — I have to go," he said, opened the door behind him and left.

"Fuck!" I shouted at the top of my lungs and then collapsed onto the couch.

Chapter 19

I didn't sleep well that night. I was preoccupied with my stalker and my inadvertent revelation to Kale. First, I decided to pay Drew a visit before I headed to the set, and second, I would have a real heart-to-heart talk with Kale and not let this one go like I did the last time. I got up early and felt anxious. I hadn't seen Drew in weeks, and I hardly knew what to say short of just making the accusation. I couldn't figure out the right way to accuse someone of stalking. If Drew was behind it, I was also worried my confrontation would not make it stop. He might get angrier and escalate his attacks. I also knew I would be forced to get a restraining order, too. Since he had also drugged me with Ecstasy to get me to sleep with him the first time (the time I betrayed Kale), I pondered if that information was still relevant. I really didn't want to dredge up all of this junk. It made me feel uncomfortable and ashamed to even consider filing a report, but I wouldn't be someone's victim either.

So I put on my best jeans and a cute knee-length T-shirt and sandals. I did care what I looked like in front of Drew. Okay, shallow, yes, but I'm a California girl, and we always want to look good even if the man who is about to see us is a stalker. That thought made me smile. Not the stalker part, just the constant need to look good. I thought I might be neurotic tinged with crazy. All right, maybe I'm not the best spokeswoman for all California girls. Well, you might have started to judge me by now anyway. I had already judged myself – and it wasn't a nice verdict. I sighed and realized it was time to be nicer to me. Maybe if I grew some confidence, I could really work things out with Kale. An all-out brutal and vulnerable exposure of my heart seemed like the next best approach versus some callous, startling confession. I dabbed some bronze lip-gloss on my lips, stood back from the bathroom mirror, smiled at my image and left.

Later on, I arrived in front of Drew's house. He had moved into a one-bedroom cottage on the north side of Los Angeles, so it was a longer drive than usual. I saw his "new" car, a Ford Focus, sitting in front of the house. A single Coast Live Oak grew in his tiny, square yard, and the patio housed a swinging loveseat. I rushed up the three steps to the patio, stepped forward and knocked on the wooden door.

A moment passed, and Drew opened the door. He was wearing long jean shorts and a black NASCAR T-shirt. He looked genuinely surprised and then pleased to see me. He opened the screen door and stepped out.

"Brea?" he said and stepped forward to hug me in a tight embrace. He was really happy to see me. "What are you doing here?"

I quickly regretted this trip. He was warm and loving – so un-Drew like. I considered what to do. Should I level the accusation? It seemed absurd right now. I grabbed his arm and pulled him over to the swing so we could sit together. It was a cool, nice morning. Drew looked at me sweetly and expectantly. He really looked healthy and attractive. My former connection came rushing back to me. I had pushed all those feelings away, and now I decided to quickly brush off this familiar rush of attraction.

"Drew, you're good?" I asked.

Drew kind of frowned a little. "Why would I not be?" he asked with a familiar anger in his voice.

Ah, there was my man. The defensiveness also felt familiar and very Drew-like. All right, now I could level off my attraction. "Hey, you know we didn't part well," I said and studied his expression. "You know, I hope you're not holding a grudge, are you?"

Drew eyed me for a moment and said, "No, Brea, no grudge. Why?"

"Good, good," I said nervously. "I'm having a bit of a problem. I didn't think it was you. I hoped not. And it seems not, but I hope you understand I needed to see you – and see your face to know. It's not you, so I'll go."

I started to get up when Drew grabbed me by the arm and pulled me back. "What are you talking about? That made no sense!"

"All right, look, I'm being stalked. Dead roses, nasty notes, and I have no idea who it is," I confessed. "I'm a little scared. I just needed to rule you out. Now I have, and I didn't come here to bother you. If it was you, I was going to ask you really nicely to stop. You were a mistake – but you were my mistake. I made our mess my mess. I could have resisted you. The truth is I didn't want to resist. I wanted you all along, too. We hurt each other, but that was enough. So, if it is you, I am asking you to stop. Please," I added softly.

I had rambled in a weird, little circle – and the expression on Drew's face reflected my meandering confession. He sat back a little in the swing and became sullen. He then looked up at me, touched my hand and slid in close. I felt the familiar sexual tension. I didn't want to feel that right now. I wished I could kill my feelings for him forever. Would I ever not feel anything for him? He didn't even deserve these feelings, which infuriated me.

"Hey, I care about you," he said. "Do you need my help? I don't know what I can do or anything, but I don't want some motherfucker to hurt you. You want me to get you a gun? I can get you a gun."

"What? No!" I said in an alarmed voice. "No! It's not that bad. I've filed a police report. No, that's a terrible suggestion. And now you've just scared me more."

Drew got a strange look on his face and sighed. "Oh, sorry. Look, whatever you need. Just ask."

I stood up, and Drew grabbed my hand. He looked up at me with the sweetest expression and said, "Good to see you, Brea."

I softened toward him, leaned over and gently kissed him good-bye. I pulled away, and we both smiled. I turned, walked away and rolled my eyes – what a crazy connection! Could I ever be within feet of Drew and not feel an undeniable pull toward him?

When I got in the car, I got a text from Lance. He was released from the hospital and asked if I would come to the apartment for dinner. I texted back that I'd come over after work. Then I looked on the production run sheet. We were filming on the Warner Bros. soundstage today. I had never been on a soundstage so I figured this would be a new adventure. When I pulled up to the security gate in my little Corolla, I felt very self-conscious. The three cars ahead of me were expensive: a Mercedes, a BMW and a Lexus. And here I was in my little Corolla. I sighed and figured someday I would have the money to upgrade, but right now I was living on the money I earned on the script. I checked in with the security shack and pulled onto the studio lot. It was not as full of hustle and bustle that day and only a few random production assistants were pulling around racks of brightly colored costumes. I soon located soundstage nine, and quietly slipped in the backdoor.

Kale and Curtis were standing around with the director, this guy who wore sunglasses even in the dark, had a head of dark, curly hair and only wore black shirts and slacks. His name was Dave, but he didn't like underlings to speak to him while he was working. So, I held back and waited until they stopped talking to approach Kale. Dave went off to talk to the camera guy, and I grabbed Kale's arm and pulled him to me.

He looked at me in surprise since I was much more assertive than usual. "Sweetheart, it's a long day … "

"Yeah, I know. Fuck it! We're going to talk tonight," I demanded. "Enough of this shit, Kale. We need to sit down – you, me, alone. I'm ready, and I can take it."

A pleased smile came over Kale's face. He kind of stood back from me a moment, studying me. "Sassy!" he said with delight. "I like it. Yeah, sweetheart, you and me tonight."

"Alone?" asked Curtis who suddenly interrupted. "What, Brea, you going to fuck with Kale some more?"

I pivoted toward Curtis and frowned. Kale also turned to Curtis and gave him a dirty look. "Dude, back the fuck off!" Kale ordered and stepped assertively toward him in an alpha-male posture.

Curtis looked from Kale to me and back to Kale again and sneered. "Well, ain't she sweet?" he said and then left us.

"I hate him," I blurted out.

Kale swung around back toward me. "Keep those feelings to yourself, sweetheart. He's your boss. Look, we'll talk tonight," he said and reached out to touch my shoulder in reassurance.

As he stepped away, I realized that if Curtis was the stalker, I would have an ugly fight on my hands. While Kale was protective of me, he wasn't prepared to trash this film over it. He loved me, but he would have me replaced with another scribe who would do the last-minute rewrites without all of the commotion and drama. I wasn't a big enough name to justify tensions with the executive producer, which was the reason I had not told Kale about my problems with Curtis in the first place. I shifted my weight back on my heels and felt more uptight than ever before.

The day went by. I mostly stayed in Kale's trailer working on a few minor revisions and notes that were sent over. I watched some of the filming, but watching my story being acted out was really strange. I kept making critical notes in my head about the bad wardrobe – a California girl wouldn't wear those clothes. The blonde actress they hired was wearing a red mini-dress with orange fringe. Ugh! It was atrocious. She also wore these sky-high platform shoes because she was super short in real life. My heroine was supposed to be tall, but Kale said there was a shortage of tall actresses around town. I kept my opinions to myself. The actress, whose name was Kelly Wilton, tried to make nice with me and pick my brain about the role. She wasn't very bright, and got all flighty talking about her "art." I listened to her ramble about art and real life and something about taking classes at theater school. I lost track of what she was actually trying to say and tuned her out.

Letty bound up to me. She had dyed her hair pink, and I wondered if it would bother the casting director. Her hair had been pumpkin orange just two days ago. "Hey," she said, "where'd you go last night?"

"Oh, sorry," I said. "Personal problems. Did you have fun?"

"Ryan's a doll. You like him or what?" she asked with a sparkle in her eyes.

"We're dating," I said. "And no, that's not an invitation to make out with him, Letty!" I said, completely straight forward.

I had after all walked in on her making out with Drew, and I figured her boundaries weren't so great. I thought a firm statement might kibosh any ulterior motives she had with my fling. I didn't much go for sharing boyfriends with my girlfriends, which she apparently didn't seem to mind.

"Cool, cool," she said and put her hands in her back pockets. "Ryan said you and this Kale guy are serious, but you keep him on the side for fun. Sounds like a plan to me, babe. Every girl should have a man in her pocket."

"Ryan's fun," I replied. "Kale's something different."

Just as I said that, Kale came up from behind me and smiled so cheerfully. He evidently liked what he had heard. "Ladies," he said and nodded at Letty. "Letty, they want you on set. Off you go."

Letty nodded and gave Kale the biggest, most flirtatiously girly smile she could muster. She then walked away with a cute swing in her ass. I knew she wasn't at all Kale's type – and I turned to look at him. He was apparently nothing more than amused by her, just as I expected. Well, Letty was amusing, so why not?

"Have you heard anything else from the police?" he seriously asked me.

"No, not yet. And no more dead roses either," I announced.

Kale nodded, smiled and took off. I watched him go. What a fantastic, perfectly sculpted ass he had. I admired it from behind. Kale must have sensed my stare because he turned a bit and caught my eyes. He had this pleased smile on his face as he carried on and began talking to the director, who still had on dark glasses and looked overly serious.

I was supposed to stop by and see Lance after work. I decided to put the talk with Kale above that stop. I would stop and see Lance afterward. Kale left the set before me, and I followed about 30 minutes behind so I could rewrite some scenes in my new script. My goal was to have script two done and ready to sell once this film ended. I wrapped up and hustled to leave. I actually felt calm about this discussion – it was long overdue. I didn't know what would happen from here, but I decided I just wanted some resolution. I didn't want to continue to hurt Kale for no good reason. He needed to see me – my authentic self. No insecurity, no fear, just confidence and honesty.

When I got to the house and through the front gates, Maya greeted me with a glass of champagne, which was a familiar gesture. "Hola, chica," she said in a thin voice.

I saw her look at me with caution and maybe some hostility. She looked down very quickly, which made me feel like she didn't want to connect with me. She was angry about Ryan. I made a mental note that we needed to spend some girl time together where I could discuss my feelings. Then again, it really wasn't any of her business, but she was protective of Kale. She didn't know what was going on, and she was on her boss' side. She had a right to choose, but I didn't want her to be angry with me either.

"Maya, maybe we can go out for drinks, huh?"

"Hmm … " she said in the same thin voice. "Kale is outside on the patio."

I nodded and walked toward the big sliding door, pulled it open and walked out. Kale was sitting on one of the chaise lounge chairs, sipping champagne and popping cheese squares into his mouth. He looked at me and smiled warmly. He didn't look at all poised for a fight. I guess he had had enough time to think about last night's revelation and cool down. But I definitely didn't think he was over it. He wasn't that flighty or detached to dismiss that kind of pain that efficiently. I saw the look on his face. He had looked like I had leveled a mortal wound, and I didn't like the hurt I caused either. Tonight, though, he seemed serene and his usual upbeat, calm self. He motioned to the lounge that was separated by a small, round table that held more champagne, cheese, crackers and grapes. I slid into the lounge and put my head back against the built-in pillow. It felt amazing. I sipped some champagne and rolled my head toward Kale.

"I know we have to do this, but what I wouldn't do to just sit here, drink and stare at your beautiful body," I said with a sigh.

"We could do that, and we could pretend some more," he said with a stiff look. "Pretend you didn't fuck me over. Pretend it didn't suck to hear it that way. I think it's time you just say whatever you came to say." He said these words so genuinely and straightforwardly. He just stared right at me and waited.

"All right. Truth time," I said, paused and sucked in air. "I can't explain Drew. It started long before we met. He followed me and did a bunch of shitty stuff – and yes, I didn't resist him. I don't want to go on and on about my feelings because I don't want to hurt you – or bore you. Drew was an addiction. I didn't want him in my life. I met you. I want you in my life. I regret all of it, I do. You've tolerated way more than you should. I am deeply sorry. I want to get past it. I don't know if it's possible. I don't know if I should even ask."

Kale sat up and shifted so his legs were out in front of me. He leaned his elbows on his knees with his hands gripped together toward me, and what he said made me sit up straight, too. "Grow the fuck up! You are so smart and talented, but emotionally … you give me this bullshit excuse about me being the one. You're too young. Total horseshit! Fucking make me your one! Or you can sell these lame excuses. I know you have a great heart – use it!"

I stared at him, shocked by his harsh words. He stared right back into my eyes, and he waited. He wasn't going to move. I got up and moved across on my knees in front of him. He looked down at me. What was there to say?

Silence and then I slowly found the words: "I love you."

And with that, Kale lurched forward in one full motion, grabbed me by the back of the neck and kissed me with such heated passion it felt bottomless. He began grabbing at my clothes with no care and ripped and pulled my dark pink blouse down, popping the tie on the front apart. I responded with the same fervor. I grabbed his back and dug my fingers into his skin. I pulled at his black shirt. He yanked my blouse all the way and swiftly threw off my bra and began hungrily kissing my breasts. His tongue licked and caressed my nipples. He sat back, looked me right in the eyes and then pulled his own shirt off. Our naked chests pressed together and seared in intoxicating warmth. He kissed my neck and around my ear. It sent shivers down my spine. I reached down to find him fully aroused and ran my fingers along the edge of his cock, rubbing up and down. I thrust my hand down his pants and found his head. I rubbed its softness on each side with the tips of my fingers. He was very hard and turned on. I pulled it open, unzipped him fast and yanked down his pants. I grasped him and this made him moan in a husky voice. He turned and pushed the lounge chair down, lay back and looked at me again right in the eyes. I eagerly moved up, easily removed my shorts and panties, grabbed his bulging cock and slid onto it.

His eyes rolled back into his head in unabashed pleasure, and he groaned deeply. He looked up at me with such lust and passion on his face. I was now on him naked and exposed. He stared at my body, sat up and began kissing my breasts again. He ran his hand down my stomach, made me quiver and let his fingers touch and rub my clit. His finger made a circular motion, and I now gasped as the tension and desire built up. I was throbbing with a burning ache. He kept rubbing, and I reached down and wrapped my hand around his cock to pleasure him as I also rode him. We were both panting and hot with pleasure.

"Say it," he whispered breathlessly.

"I want you," I responded without hesitation.

He then slid all the way down and stared up at me. I leaned forward and started kissing him and rocking up and down on his big, hard cock. I jerked up just a little to meet his eyes. We stared right at each other. We both were hardly able to focus it felt so amazing. I was so happy to be making love with him – finally. My hips began moving as he kept moving his hands and massaging my ass. Our eyes stayed locked as I rocked on top of him. As I moved in a steady rhythm, he moaned in ecstasy; he reached up and grabbed me and pulled me into a long, sensual kiss. The very tip of his tongue reached into my mouth, and I responded in-kind. I kissed and thrust very deeply into him as far and as hard as I could manage. I felt him all the way inside of me, and I was so excited and focused on the intensity of the pleasure.

"Harder," he urged in a whisper.

I rocked him even faster. He was kissing and staring at me. "Oh god!" he moaned and our eyes fixed. "Yes!" he shouted and I moved and thrust as hard as I could. He began rapidly thrusting over and over, and he finally lost control and began to orgasm. As he did, he managed to fix his eyes on me, and his intense stare just made me lose it. I felt extreme pleasure. I couldn't stand it. The minute he came, I joined him. We were both moaning and maintaining our stare. I quivered as I came over and over in the most intense multiple orgasms. My leg muscles were weak, and I collapsed against his chest, breathing heavily as my body started to tremble. Kale wrapped his long arms all the way around my body and held me very close to him. I started to cry silently as tears rolled down my cheeks. I hugged him even harder. He must have felt the tears spilling onto his perfectly hairy chest. He kissed my forehead very tenderly.

"I love you, sweetheart," he whispered in my ear.

I cried silently some more. I then allowed myself to look him in the eyes, raising my head to expose my teary eyes. He reached up and gently swiped the tears off my face, pulled me into a kiss and then pulled away. He tenderly brushed a hair off my cheek.

"I love you, too," I added quietly.

I decided to stay the night with Kale. He felt safe and secure, and I would be protected from my stalker. I texted Lance and told him I would come by in the morning to visit. He was okay with it and admitted he felt tired anyway. I didn't tell him I was back with Kale. We lay in the cool of the lounge chair for about an hour, sipped champagne and ate cheese and crackers. We talked about how well the movie was going, and how it was on budget. Movies couldn't afford to go over budget in this economy, as Kale so expertly pointed out. As I listened to the soft lilt of his voice, I felt incredibly comfortable to be home in his arms. It was right as I realized I was safe with him that I decided to discuss Curtis.

I worked up the nerve to tell him about Curtis' proposition to manage my career and his inference that he would manage "me" as well. Kale listened with concern on his face. I admitted I was scared to tell him since it might cause trouble on the set. He sat up and looked me straight in the eyes.

"I would never let anyone hurt you! Tell me what you want me to do and I'll take care of Curtis," he offered as he reached out and touched my face in reassurance. "I know this happens all of the time, but one word and I'll take him out. You think he's sending the dead roses?"

I looked down and felt uncomfortable about my knight riding to my rescue. "Please don't go all alpha on me. Just let me handle him," I pleaded. "I don't know if he's sending the crap. I'll talk to him with you there. Okay, and no fights. I don't want that either."

"I'll get you a proper manager all right," offered Kale. "I'll call my friend Stewart. He's a good guy, and he knows everyone around town. But what I was really thinking is that I want to be a team. Writer and producer – what do you think?"

I leaned up and kissed him. "Can I think about it?"

"Of course, sweetheart" he replied. "Now I am thinking about other things," he grinned at me.

"When aren't you?" I asked and slid down the length of his chest.

He grinned with great satisfaction at me. I began giving him head. I wrapped my mouth around his big, hard cock, ran my tongue up and down his shaft. He moaned and enjoyed all of it. I licked him up and down. His hand came to rest on top of my blonde hair and he kept moaning with each deep thrust into my throat. He liked it when I did this. He told me later it was his favorite thing. I licked him excessively like a lollipop, and he grew very hard. I quickly jumped on top of him to ride him. I pushed long and deep into him. Then I grabbed his hand and rested it on my nub and showed him how to move it, teaching him what felt hot to me. He obliged and let me move his hand until I moved away and bent forward to kiss his hairy chest and find his nipples. I found one and with my mouth, I bit down a bit. This made him cry in pleasure and pain. He liked it. I sucked and kissed and bit.

He tried to continue to focus his motion on me, but I could tell the kissing and sucking was a bit too distracting. I ran my mouth up his chest to his neck and ears where I kissed his lobe. He just couldn't take this anymore. He growled like an animal and forced himself to pleasure me to ensure I came, too (such a gentleman). That was no problem because I was so turned on it was inevitable. He came first and then I just lost all control and screamed over and over again as the ripple of the orgasm fluttered through my body.

We eventually went up to the house and crawled in bed where we made love twice and fell asleep. We both had to get up early. As I rested in the nook of his arm, I thought about how great he felt. I wondered what my problem was that it took me this long to return "home" to my lover. I decided I wasn't going to analyze the relationship or worry where it was or was not going. We were just going to be. Kale liked that idea. No pressure and no expectations. He even went so far as to suggest I maintain my relationship with "Ry-Ry," only without the sexual favors. I snickered that I suspected Ryan wasn't capable of friendship with women. I liked Ryan, though, and I would talk to him. I thought it showed a lot of trust that Kale even made the suggestion. I snuggled him. I knew it was okay again.

The next morning I got up to find Kale had left a note. He had an early call and had already left for the set. He told me to grab breakfast and take my time. I lay in bed and stared out the window toward the yard where I could see a single palm tree. I was surprised to see it was overcast and slightly raining. It was early fall, and LA only got a little bit of rain each year. I thought it would smell fresh when I went outside. I loved that first rain smell. I got up, showered and headed downstairs. As I got to the edge of the stairs, I looked around for Maya – she was nowhere in sight but a big tray of fresh fruit, muffins and coffee was sitting out. I had hoped to speak with her before I left to see Lance, but she either wasn't there or was avoiding me. I pulled up a barstool at the center kitchen counter, grabbed a blueberry muffin, poured coffee with a touch of cream and quietly ate alone. I kept looking out toward the yard and the damp pavement. I loved fall, but in LA there was no discernable change in the seasons. It was perpetually green. I missed the seasons.

After I ate the muffin and finished my coffee, I decided to move along. I scooted out the door and left in my Corolla to see Lance before work. I pulled into the familiar parking complex and headed up to his apartment with a skip in my step. When I had gone outside, I had smelled exactly what I had expected – fresh, damp pavement and greenery. It smelled much the same outside of Lance's apartment. I knocked on the door and Lance opened it. He looked much healthier and even rosy cheeked again, but he still wore a red dew rag to cover his hairless head. This sight made me so happy. I rushed into his arms and hugged him tight. He hugged me with the same affection. We walked all the way in, and Lance offered me more coffee, which I accepted, knowing I would be amped up on caffeine and all set for work. I was sure to be a little zinged out and a touch manic – what a thought.

"You look much, much better," I told him with a smile.

"I'm okay," he replied. "They think they can get this thing into remission. I might even be able to go back to work," he said and sighed. "It's boring around here, and I'm tired of being in bed. But you know what? I don't want to talk about it. How's the movie?"

"Wow! Weird and fun," I replied. "I've got a stalker," I admitted plainly.

"A what? What?" Lance turned and frowned at me. "Brea?"

"Oh, to heck with it," I replied. "I'm handling it."

Lance handed me coffee from the kitchen and leaned on the counter across from me. I had taken a seat at the stool next to the built-in shelf that opened into the kitchen.

"I'm going to Fiji," said Lance out the blue. "You want to go? My treat?"

"Fiji?" I asked. "When?"

"At the end of the month to celebrate the end of chemo," he said.

"Wow! That's generous and cool of you," I replied. "But … "

"But … "

"I'm back with Kale, and I don't think he would like it," I admitted.

Lance looked disappointed and sad. He became pensive and quiet for a second. "You think it will last this time?"

"I'm not asking those questions."

"Is he?" Lance gave me a look.

"Not yet," I said with a sigh. "We're just together. I don't want to think about anything more than that right now. This movie is in production. I have another script I'm writing. And that's that."

Lance walked from around the counter and stood in front of me. He reached out and pulled me off the stool. He wrapped his arms all the way around me. He just held me for a few minutes. He then pulled away and placed a sweet kiss on my mouth. It was nice and soft and not meant to seduce me.

"If you find your stalker, tell me," he said. "I'll kick his ass."

"Well, thank you. Good to know," I said and laughed. "You know what we ought to do?"

"No, what?"

"Skydive! You haven't lived till you've jumped out of a plane," I offered with a laugh. "Or heck, climb Mount Everest! Or just cross the Andes. You almost died!"

Lance began to laugh. "I'll let you know which one, but only if you go with me!"

"All right, " I responded. "Now I have to go to work. You look so much better. And I'm glad. Love you," I said, hugging him one more time before I pulled away and headed to the door. I turned once more. We looked at each other. I waved, smiled and exited.

I walked outside and stopped dead in my tracks – a living red rose was now shoved under my windshield wiper. I hesitantly walked up, grabbed it and stared. What did this mean? The person had not left a note this time – and the rose wasn't dead. I stared at it and then threw it to the ground. I didn't like it – alive or dead. Someone had followed me … again. I decided to tell Kale later on when I saw him. "Fuck!" I said quietly under my breath and got into my car.

Chapter 20

Later on, I returned to Kale's on-set trailer to meet him. When I got there, I opened the door and found Curtis sitting on the sofa. He was reading something on his iPad and looked up. I stopped dead in my tracks and stared at him. In my surprise, I had left the door open.

"Here, let me get that for you," Curtis offered as he set down the iPad on the coffee table, got up and pulled the door shut.

It slammed a little and startled me. Curtis stood there and looked at me. "Why so jumpy?"

"Huh? No, I'm fine. Maybe I should go find Kale," I said nervously. I didn't want to be alone with him.

"Kale went to a meeting about a new project," he said.

"Oh, um, maybe I should wait outside."

"Why do that?" he asked and frowned.

Curtis didn't move back to the sofa. He loomed over me and looked at me with a strange glint in his eyes. He stepped forward, and I stepped back. He then conveniently reached around me and locked the door with a "click." I glanced at his hand that now swiftly reached across and grabbed me by the shoulders.

"Come sit down," he urged. "You look tense."

He firmly pushed me toward the sofa and down onto the brown velour cushion. I sat there stiffly as he moved around me and sat behind me. He began to try to rub my shoulders. "I give a great massage," he said.

I pulled away from him and turned so I could face him. "Don't," I said. "I don't need a massage."

Curtis leaned forward so that he was too close. I shifted backward to avoid the feel of his hot breath. "I know what you need," he said and lurched at me to kiss my neck. I completely jumped away and fell onto the ground. Curtis dived forward and his entire body was covering me. He was turned on.

I tried to wriggle out from underneath him and cried out, "Get the fuck off me!"

He smothered his face into my neck and began kissing me. I shoved at him, which only encouraged him more. "You know you want this."

"No, no I don't! Get off or I'm going to scream!" I cried out.

"These trailers are soundproof, go ahead," he retorted and reached under my purple, cotton dress and groped my crotch.

I realized I was in deep trouble and cried out. He kept groping me as he pinned me down. I tried to roll around and grasped at the carpet to pull out from under him. Just then, I heard the door click – someone was trying to enter.

"Help!" I screamed, and Curtis grabbed me by the mouth to stop me.

He started to pull back and get off me. Just as he yanked me into his chest with his hand over my mouth, the door swung open – it was Kale. Kale's eyes widened, and he reached down to grab Curtis' collar and yank him off of me. Kale was able to fully pull him away and pushed him over to the edge of the trailer so he could get to me. He leaned over and pulled me up, holding me very close to his chest as he swung around to glare at Curtis.

"Curtis, what the fuck?" Kale yelled. "You're a rapist now?"

"I didn't rape her," he retorted.

Kale helped me sit down, and then he turned on Curtis. "She told me you've been bothering her. What the fuck am I supposed to do? She could sue us."

"She won't sue," he replied with spite. "You're not going to shut us down over this little bitch."

Kale moved forward and with one swift punch, he clocked Curtis who reeled against the wall. "Who's the bitch?"

Curtis grasped his swollen cheek, glared at us and headed toward the door. "And if you're the one sending the flowers that better stop!" warned Kale.

Curtis looked first over at me and then at Kale and asked, "What the hell are you talking about, man?"

"Get the fuck out of here!" yelled Kale.

I was completely shocked and fell back onto the sofa. Kale rushed over to comfort me. "You okay?"

My hips hurt from being held down on the hard ground as I tried to escape. "He's an asshole!" I suddenly said. "Are you going to fire him?"

Kale sat up a bit in alarm. "Sweetheart, I can't fire him. He financed 25 percent of this film."

I withdrew into myself. Kale, my lover and defender; I had found his chink. "So, what am I supposed to do? Just let him get away with attacking me?"

"I'll keep him away from you, I promise," he offered in such a lame way.

I sat there quietly and took this all in. I shifted and looked into my lover's light blue-green eyes. He looked worried. I wondered if he was worried about me or his beloved film. I didn't like what I was thinking. I wanted to shout at him or maybe I just wanted to scream at Curtis. I felt confused and angry. I thought this sort of thing happened primarily to actresses on casting couches – at least that was the ugly myth. I guessed a lowly writer wasn't immune. I sat back against the sofa and stared helplessly at Kale. Kale sensed my fear and alienation. He pulled me to him.

"What can I do?" he asked softly.

"Nothing, but what if he's dead-rose guy? And P.S., it was a live rose this morning."

"What?" he asked.

I told him about this morning's gift. He said he felt certain it wasn't Curtis since he had been on set since 5:00 a.m. I just listened and felt numb. Welcome to the ugly underground reality of world-famous Tinseltown. Kale just kept looking at me with a worried, furrowed brow of concern. I knew he was unsettled about the possibility that I might sue the entire movie, which I didn't want to do. I also didn't want to mention it. He would know it was on my mind and get more anxious. Kale explained that he had known Curtis for the last five years, and he didn't know this side of him. They had produced three movies together. He never acted out with other women that he knew about. I reiterated, "That he 'knew' about."

When I asked why Curtis had even offered to manage me when he was not a manager, Kale seemed perplexed by that one. He acknowledged that maybe Curtis intended to manage talent, too. I thought it was all crap and said as much. The more we talked, the more I realized he wasn't going to do anything more about Curtis than he already had. The gauntlet had been thrown down, and now at least Curtis knew that Kale was in on his ploys. Kale did say he would talk to him privately when I left.

I felt a wedge come between us. Kale wasn't at all saying what I wanted to hear. Why wasn't he ready to protect me? Did he have too much at stake? Maybe after what I had done, our relationship wasn't worth it. These feelings dredged up shame and guilt. I wanted to cast myself in the role of femme fatale, which just made me inwardly laugh at how ridiculous that idea seemed. I wouldn't make a very good martyr; I was too busy feeling angry now toward Curtis – and Kale for finally having a sign of weakness. I loved his near-perfect image. Now it was smeared a little, and I was just simmering about it.

Kale sensed my feelings and looked straight at me. "You know, you need a break – we'll go away to Santa Barbara. I have a beachfront estate where we can chill."

Was he trying to soothe my feelings with beach time? I nodded and looked down. Kale scooted in and leaned over so he could look at me. "Don't be upset. It will be fine."

I surged with the desire to whine like a petulant child that I was pissed and upset with him for not protecting me. I just couldn't offer any positive feelings right then. The negative was overshadowing how I felt about all of this. I had a gnawing and vague uncertainty about what was going on. Kale grabbed my whole body and pulled me onto his lap. I was still in a seated position, so he grabbed my legs, spread them and made me wrap them around him so that I faced him. He looked serious and concerned.

"Lover … don't brood," he urged.

I felt indignant that my violation and confusion came across to him as sulking. I wanted to slap him, fuck him and leave. Aggression and passion swirled inside of me like a cataclysmic storm of emotions. "You think I'm sulking? I just got attacked, Kale!"

Justice! I wanted justice. Kale studied my expression for a moment. He was searching for an emotional connection to understand me – to maybe understand what I wanted, which he either wouldn't or couldn't give me.

"What do you expect?" he finally asked.

I studied his expression and searched his intense eyes. All answers led somewhere that would hurt him or me. I could have gone the route of self-preservation and put yet another rift between us. I knew my only choice without nuking our relationship was to relent. I had to care more about his feelings – his situation – than my rage, anger and violation. So I did the typically female thing. I gave up a fight I couldn't win without losing something precious.

"Nothing," I finally replied in a tepid voice.

Kale leveled one last gaze at me when a knock came to the door, and he was called to set to watch the dailies. He stared at me for a moment longer, sizing me up. He then leaned in and met my gaze. We stayed locked in a fixed mutual stare. He then tenderly kissed me for a very long time – almost two minutes.

When he finished, he stared at me one more time, leaned in and whispered, "I love you, all right."

I nodded and accepted this as some sort of denouement to this whole mess – act three of our conflict. And like many women confronted with sexual politics, I would not get my justice. Kale, whose connection to me now was so strong, sensed my thoughts. He had this sad look for a moment and then told me he had to go – and he would come stay at my apartment tonight. I felt relieved not to go home alone. My stalker was still out there, and that was yet another problem to solve.

Chapter 21

Before I headed home, Ryan called me and asked if I wanted to meet him for lemonade – hard lemonade at this place called the Lemon Shack. I agreed since I thought this would be the time to shift the gears in our relationship. I told Kale to meet me back at my apartment later that night. He didn't react at all when I told him I was going to see Ryan.

So, I parked my car up the street from the Lemon Shack, which was this open-air building with white walls that contained huge pictures of close-ups of lemons and lemon trees. The bar itself was a shelf that sat in front of a gigantic floor-to-ceiling window with the usual counter situated three feet in front of it. Ryan was sitting on a silver-padded barstool, laughing and chatting with the female bartender who wore a tight, cleavage-showing, white spandex dress. I sat down and admired her, too. She was pretty sexy. I was sure her breasts were silicone, but they looked amazing. Ryan managed to peel his gaze off her bodacious body and smiled really big at me.

"Hey, babe!" he said and gave me an open hug. He then sweetly kissed me and pulled away since I didn't let the kiss linger. He kind of frowned at that, but then being Ryan and easygoing, he shrugged it right off. "Layla, please get my lady a tall one," he requested.

"I don't drink beer," I interrupted.

Layla smiled and said, "We don't serve beer."

"Huh?" I replied.

Ryan just nodded at Layla and said, "You'll see, babe."

No sooner had he said that and Layla placed a tall, slim glass filled with yellow liquid in front of me. Ryan nodded for me to go ahead, and I took a sip. "Whoa!" I said between clenched teeth. "That's strong!"

Ryan laughed. "Sip it," he urged.

I proceeded to tell Ryan my latest set of problems, including the stalking and the situation with Curtis. Ryan's leg kept tapping up and down. He had so much energy I could tell it was hard from him to stay focused or sit still. He did listen attentively and then whistled between his teeth as he drank his own hard lemonade. The Killer's "Hot Fuss" was playing in the background.

"I also have some other news," I said as I prepared to tell him about Kale.

"You're fucking Kale again," he said in a disinterested voice.

"How'd you know?" I asked.

"Johnny said you two seemed tight. It's cool, Brea. I think you're awesome! You're the first chick I ever got to jump out of a plane with me," he said with a smirk. "And I started to think we could go somewhere, but then I'd have to give up the black book. So you know, we can still mess around. I'm good with that."

I nodded and thought about his candor. He was a straightforward guy so I didn't think he was hiding his feelings. I decided to change the subject. "All right, what the heck is the deal with Johnny? You're friends, then you're not, and now you're friends again?"

Ryan shifted toward me and asked, "You really want the nasty truth?"

"Yes," I said.

"My dad propositioned him," he said.

My jaw dropped. Ryan nodded. "What? Your dad's gay?"

"Gay, bi, who knows. Dad's kind of a weird guy. I didn't believe Johnny. So, there you go."

"And you do now?" I asked.

Ryan shrugged. "Yeah, after my dad got caught in a bathhouse with some other dude and had to pay off the reporter to shut the fuck up. I had to pick him up from jail. It blew, man. So, I had to suck it up with Johnny. Can't trust dear old dad, I guess."

I sat there quietly processing this confession. Poor Ryan. He seemed to handle it okay, but I would imagine no son wants to find out his dad propositioned a friend – male or female. The whole time Ryan told me his confession, he kept his eyes down as he rolled a packet of sugar back and forth along the bar. I leaned against his arm.

"I'm sorry," I said in a low voice. "Family can be so disappointing."

"This town is loaded with disappointments," he said rather

dryly. He shifted toward me and tilted his head in a flirtatious way. "God, I wish you weren't all shacked up again," he lamented and then leaned over and kissed me. "What a waste of great tail."

"If I was way more liberal, I would keep you as a lover," I admitted with a laugh. "I happen to know for a fact that Kale won't go for that one."

And with that, Kale came up from behind and touched me right under my breast. I turned in surprise to see him. He wrapped his arms around me from behind, snuggled against my neck and smiled warmly at Ryan, who looked surprised, too.

"You don't mind, do you Ry-an?" He said Ryan's name with that slight mock that Ryan didn't notice. I did, though.

Ryan extended his hand and shook Kale's in a friendly way and then jumped off the barstool. "No man, she's all yours."

Kale smiled and kissed my cheek. "You don't have to go," he said as he looked up from my neck.

"Nah, I got my black book, no problem, babe. You kids have fun," he said and then darted off.

Kale took Ryan's place at the bar, waved to Layla and ordered what I was having. Then all of his laser-beam attention shifted to me. "You're right," he said.

"About what?" I asked and took another sip of my drink.

"Kale not liking that," he said in a sarcastic tone.

"Ah, come on, you're not jealous, are you?" I asked. "And you're not checking up on me, too? Please say no."

Kale sighed and smiled at me. "I'm worried about you, sweetheart. Besides, I needed a drink," he said and picked up his glass and took a surprisingly big gulp. "Do I need to check up on you?" he asked and shifted his eyes so we were looking at each other.

"You know what?" I asked and slid forward on my stool so I could whisper in a low voice. "Let's get drunk and fuck. We can call your driver, what do you say?"

Kale turned toward me, gave me this very sexy smile and picked up his glass. "Cheers then," he said and held out his glass.

I picked up my own, and we toasted. I took a much bigger swig this time, ordered water to prevent a hangover and asked for a second glass. We relaxed and just let it all go. The worry and anxiety of the day washed away with every drink of liquor-infused lemonade. I made sure I balanced each drink with a matching gulp of water. We sat very close to each other and talked more about Curtis. Kale told me he had spoken to him. He swore Curtis would leave me alone. I wasn't sure I believed him, but he really seemed upset about it, not just for me, but also for us.

"This is a fantastic business; I love it! But you know it's littered, too; all business is really," he said. "You're a beauty. Men will try shit. Don't be naïve about it, and you'll get by. And enjoy the fun. Are you even having fun?" he suddenly asked.

I shifted a moment and thought about it. I smiled and leaned toward him, "Yes, please."

He laughed boisterously at this admission. I could tell he was getting loaded. The tension lifted from his furrowed brow.

"Maybe you should write a book, too," he suddenly said.

"Maybe," I replied and took another drink. I then leaned forward and wrapped each arm around his neck and pulled him into a kiss. I could taste the sweet and strong taste of the alcohol in his mouth and on his tongue. We took a long, deep kiss. Kale kissed so perfectly, so sensually. He pulled away and gazed at me. His blue-green eyes were intense and could draw me in and turn me on – just one look. He was a strong, level, decent guy. He kind of reeked of his authentic honesty and sweet humility. Maybe it was his open face and eyes; but he came across like it was impossible for him to lie. The Killer's "Change Your Mind" played right at that moment. I felt a swirl of lust, intoxication and relaxation flow over my mind. I reached up and ran my fingers through his blonde hair and brushed fine strands back and away. Kale closed his eyes and enjoyed the sensation.

"Can we get naked now?" he asked with his eyes still closed.

I looked over at his second glass. "You need another and then we'll go."

Kale grabbed me by the waist. His eyes were now open as he pulled me closer and leaned over so he could inhale my smell. "Sweet," he sighed. He stared at me. "Are you thinking about my offer? Writer-producer team?"

"Easy there, hero," I cautioned and took another drink. "Let's finish this film first."

Kale nodded. "I admire your caution. I'm all jump and go. But we should take it slow. You're right."

"You're all jump ... on me – and that's all right," I said in a soft voice with a huge smile and a slow, seductive nod of approval.

The driver arrived a short time later to pick us up. We rode back in the Town Car. We each sat down in our respective seats, stared at each other and then Kale reached across and pushed me down on the seat so we could kiss.

Kale whispered "no touching" when I went to put my hands down his pants. I quickly obeyed and followed his lead. We did nothing but kiss all the way home.

We got back to his house and tumbled in the door, laughing and giggling into the house. We went straight upstairs. I walked in ahead of Kale, turned around and stood there. He walked through the French doors and just stood in front of me, enjoying the staring game.

"Strip for me," he said with this grin of pleasure.

I leveled my gaze right into his eyes. First, I removed my purple gauze dress, held it in one hand, extended my arm out and dropped it to the floor. "Your turn," I ordered in a soft voice and never blinked.

"Oh now, it's tit for tit," he said with a laugh.

Of course, his joke made me smile. Kale maintained the same stare and slowly unbuttoned each button on his blue shirt, pulled his sleeves off and did the exact same gesture, holding it out and dropping it. He nodded for me to go next. I reached behind and undid my black bra and off it went to the ground. The rules were now understood. Kale yanked off his black leather belt and then suddenly stepped forward and playfully folded it over and pretended to hit me on the ass, but he was gentle and it barely touched me. He removed his slacks and now stood inches from me – and his manhood was bulging and stretching out his white Calvin's. I was so turned on; it took all I could manage not to touch him.

His stare never wavered and he nodded for me to continue. I took off my right black stiletto and then the other one. I nodded at him. He removed his Calvin's, and with one swift yank, he turned me and bent me over the bed. I felt his fingertips go down the length of my back, which sent a chill through my body and made my hair stand straight up on end. He then reached up to my neck and brushed my hair forward so it covered my face. He seemed to enjoy each touch and savor it with slow enthusiasm. He kept running his fingertips down to my ass and stopped. He then leaned forward and kissed me on the back of my neck with extreme tenderness. I was so turned on and just waited to let him guide me through the experience.

He kissed me all the way down my back, and as he did so, he reached both arms around and caressed my breasts. Sometime while he was touching and distracting me, he must have found his remote control for the stereo and Mat Kearney's song "Breathe In and Breathe Out" infused the air. Then I felt something cool on my back. He had also managed to find massage oil. The man was magical. He had kept me engaged in pleasure with one hand while doing stuff with the other. He rubbed the oil in his own hands first to warm it up, and then he rested his hands gently on my back and slowly began to massage first my shoulders and then my back in long circular strokes.

I sighed and closed my eyes and listened to Radio Head's "Fake Plastic Tree" lyrics, which had replaced Mat Kearney. In the lead singer's falsetto voice, the words echoed in my head. Kale rubbed the oil all over my back, and I was lost in the beauty of the music and the sensuality of his hands. And just like the song suggested about the lover being worn out, I realized that was exactly how I felt. I was intoxicated and floating away into the sensations of the moment. I became a ragdoll in Kale's large hands as he turned me over onto the bed. He looked down into my eyes, and I could see the sweetest smile creep across his face.

I closed my eyes again and allowed myself to be swept away between sensuality and bliss, and we drifted away in the rhythm. He had me stretched out across the bed, and he crept over me like a shadow slowly engulfing my body in his. I could feel him hover over me and wait. His hands massaged my breasts and slowly moved down and rubbed and caressed me. I arched my back into him. He used his fingers at first to enter me. I moaned and wanted him so bad it physically made me ache. I opened my eyes – and he was watching me. He was enjoying watching my reactions and lustfulness.

"Now look at me," he said softly. "Just watch me."

I obeyed and kept my eyes on him. He slowly lowered into me and penetrated. I sucked in air, my eyes fluttered in pleasure; I was having a difficult time maintaining my stare, but he was completely fixated on me. His gaze never moved from my face, and he carefully watched my expression. Every flutter, every eye movement and reaction in my face turned him on. He began to fuck me harder and a little rougher. I reached around and grabbed his ass and pushed him as deeply into me as I could. It almost hurt from how large he was, but pleasure and pain became intensely entwined in excitement. I wanted to maintain my gaze, but I couldn't, the pleasure was building and throbbing. I pushed up again so I could rub against his groin. He smiled a little at me. He was enjoying my reaction as much as I was. I began to feel the release coming close. God, it felt amazing. I gasped and then a scream of pure pleasure came in synch with my multiple orgasms. Kale looked extremely pleased.

When I had settled a bit, he leaned over and whispered, "My turn."

He began rapidly thrusting into me, almost pounding me, but in a pleasing way. I was so relaxed, and I put my arms over my head, closed my eyes and listened to his breathing. He was panting, and then he let go of a groan that sounded almost painful. He came and fell on top me and then gently rolled off. We lay side by side for a moment. The next song "Heaven Forbid" by the Fray played in the background. Kale turned his head to the side so he could stare at me. Our eyes met. He sweetly smiled, grabbed my hand, raised it to his mouth and kissed it.

"I love you," he said quietly while continuing to look at me.

I nodded, leaned into him and kissed him on those tulip-shaped lips. "I love you, too."

Chapter 22

I went home the next morning very early. I felt great. We had an amazing night together. Kale was still asleep when I left. I did find a note on the counter from Maya who asked me to have drinks with her that night. I was surprised we were even on good terms. She had been so hostile lately. When I got back to my apartment, Denise was sitting in the kitchen area drinking coffee and making her lunch for the day. She looked up at me and smiled.

"Well hello, stranger!" she exclaimed and took a sip out of her mug. "Where have you been?"

"I stayed at Kale's," I replied. "You got some coffee for me?"

Denise proceeded to open a cupboard, pull out a white mug, pour some coffee and splash some cream in it. She handed it to me as I stepped forward.

"Any more calls?" I asked and knew she would understand the question.

"No, not the last few days," she replied. "Any more dead flowers?"

"No, only a live one," I said.

Denise nodded thoughtfully and said, "Hmm, sounds promising."

"I suppose," I replied.

"Your dad called," she said suddenly. "He wants to know if you're coming home for Thanksgiving."

I nodded and considered the idea but didn't reply to Denise, who said she was going home for sure. She asked if I wanted to join her. My relationship with my family was always messy, tense and uncomfortable. I preferred to stay away and avoid the whole situation as much as possible. My parents were religious, uptight Protestants. They really didn't approve of my lifestyle and the whole holiday would be spent with my mother telling me to come home and take a job at the local paper. I shuddered at the thought. Denise said she and her new boyfriend, some guy named Jeremiah who she had met while grocery shopping at Whole Foods, was going with her. She had ended things with her boss Tom Jones when she found out he was now doing the file clerk. I hadn't met Jeremiah yet. She said he was vegan and totally insisted on Tofurkey, which made me laugh.

"How are you going to get your family to prepare Tofurkey?" I asked. Denise's family was an all-American, beef-eating bunch that was originally from Texas. Asking them to make Tofurkey was like asking a lion to eat lettuce sprigs over wildebeest.

She shrugged, grinned and said, "Cross that bridge when I get there. I have to get to work." She walked past me and reached out and rubbed my shoulder with affection. She paused, smiled and said, "You look really good," and then she kissed and hugged me good-bye.

"Thanks, sweetie," I replied. I did feel good. Things were still somewhat unresolved, but at least Kale was back in my life. I felt like I could deal with the rest of it as long as I had some support.

I arrived on the set later on while they were setting up a shot on the soundstage. Johnny and his costar, Kelly Wilton, were talking quietly together. Some of the extras were milling around the craft services table, eating and talking. I noticed Kelly's costume was the infamous "Love My Coconuts" dress, which made me smile. Letty had told me earlier that they had asked her to retrieve a dress from the shop. The film version was loosely based on my escapades, but carefully left out my relationship with Kale. I also never revealed to Kale just how autobiographical the script had been before all of the rewrites. I also had managed to turn most of the truth into fictional accounts that masked reality.

As I was standing there, I felt a hand on my shoulder and turned to find Curtis. I pulled protectively away from him. He held out his hand and said, "Truce."

I looked from his hand to his placid face and stayed away. I folded my arms. "Yeah, all right. Is Kale here yet?"

Curtis shook his head and looked over at Johnny and Kelly. "They're getting along," he said with a sort of smug smile on his face. "Wasn't he one of your boy toys?"

"No, we're friends. And that's none of your business," I spat at him.

Curtis, who was much taller, made it feel like he was looming over me. "Better watch that," he warned. "Don't forget I'm your boss," he said as his right eyebrow arched and he folded his arms.

I turned to fully face him and said, "As my boss, you are not entitled to touch me or ask about my personal life. And I don't want you as my manager, so don't ask again," I said and paused. "To be clear."

Curtis glared at me and then leaned over so he couldn't be heard and whispered, "You better keep Kale happy ... babe!" He looked right into my eyes. He then turned, stepped away and strolled over to Johnny and Kelly to chat.

Johnny glanced over at me and waved. I nodded. He looked back at Kelly and then I knowingly smiled. He was doing her – that look on his face said it all. I chuckled. What the hell? They were both single and available. I also noticed Kelly reached out and touched the upper part of Johnny's arm – an intimate, personal gesture. Yes, they were involved. Just as I smiled, I felt Kale's familiar hand touch the small of my back. I turned and smiled widely at him. I was happy to see him.

"Kelly and Johnny are fucking," I whispered the secret.

Kale looked over at them. Kelly was now standing super close to Johnny in his personal space. Kale nodded, looked at me and then said, "You're absolutely right."

"Is that going to be problem?" I asked.

"Only if they make it one," he replied back. "The publicity will be great for the film. Tabloid trash for sure," he said with a knowing look.

"Which is why I like the behind-the-scenes work," I replied.

"Oh, sweetheart, you don't want to be famous?" he asked and eyed me. "You would look amazing on *Maxim,*" he said with a grin.

I playfully pushed his arm. "No, I don't want to be famous. I don't want paparazzi to photograph me while I eat breakfast or grab a cup of coffee. Or snap a close-up of cellulite on my thigh. God, I hate that shit!" I replied.

"Paparazzi, sweetheart, are the true scum of the earth. They would photograph actors on the shitter if they could," said Kale as he looked off into the distance, nodded, turned and kissed me. "I have to go. See you tonight?"

"Yep," I replied and watched my handsome boyfriend move quickly off toward the director who had joined the discussion with Johnny, Kelly and Curtis. My work on the script was pretty much done at this point. They still sent over the occasional adjustments, but not many major changes. I had long ago shifted my focus to my new script. I was about to leave when I felt someone come in from behind me. I turned around and was surprised to find Monica. She had been working on another script for Kale and had been virtually ignoring this film and me. I was startled, jumped a little and touched my chest to feel my heart pounding. Monica, who was wearing blue glasses, sort of looked at me with boredom and I thought maybe a hint of disdainfulness.

"Hi," she said simply. "Things okay over here?" she asked

and looked me up and down, which bothered me.

She was such a cryptic character to figure out. I didn't know if she liked or hated me. She rarely spoke to me, and she still shadowed Kale whenever he was close. I thought I might probe her a little. "Hey, so do you have a boyfriend?" I asked trying to act nonchalant and casual.

"Boyfriend?" She gave me the strangest look — one like she might be disgusted by the question, thought or both. "No," she said. "You and Kale looked cozy the other day."

"So?" I replied and decided I would not confide in her.

She turned, looked at me a little shiftily and replied, "Yeah, so what, huh." She then sort of got this dry smile on her face and walked away. What did that mean? I pondered it for a moment. Was she or wasn't she after Kale? She had a strange interest in him. I couldn't put my finger on it, but something seemed off with her. She walked over to the group now gathered around the monitor looking at the replay of a scene. She stood close to Kale like she usually did, looked down and clearly wasn't interested in watching the monitor. After a moment, she managed to pull Kale aside and talk quietly to him. I watched this scene more like a member of an audience, scrutinizing her. I saw Kale briefly glance in my direction, smile a little and look back down.

I got a text later from Maya asking me to meet her in Santa Monica at some seafood shack called The Hungry Cat. She said she wanted cracked crab and to talk to me. I agreed to meet her at 6:00 p.m. I drove about an hour in heavy LA traffic, parked about a mile back from the restaurant and walked all the way in. It was dusk and slightly hazy as I walked and felt the slight chill of another autumn coastal night in the air. The sun was setting, and the sky was lit in faint pink – it was stunning.

When I arrived, Maya was sitting back against a big picture window. She looked completely radiant against the darkening, pinkish sky. The crash of the ocean faintly roared in the background as I sat down. The waiter brought water, and I relaxed into the chair.

"You still mad at me?" I suddenly asked.

"Muy," she said in a dark tone.

"I'm back with Kale. I don't know why you got so involved in it, Maya."

"You didn't see him. All sad without you," she replied. "He would come home and sit on the patio for hours and say nothing. Not like my Kale. You hurt him, muy malo."

"What?" I asked completely shocked by the admission. I had no idea it had been that terrible for Kale. I felt worse than ever. I wasn't used to someone loving me so deeply. Maybe I just wasn't used to love at all. Kale's protective nature and his tenderness were unfamiliar. I was always so selfishly focused on my feelings that I hadn't recognized that Kale was much more hurt than I had realized. He had such a cool, controlled way about him. He was a gentle, playful and sensitive man.

"You going to stay together now or you go fuck another gringo?" she asked harshly.

The waiter interrupted our conversation by pouring

water into our glasses and asking to take our orders. I noticed he was cookie-cutter handsome and figured he was probably an actor. He kind of glanced down at me, which made me smile, and he reciprocated. This minor flirtation only seemed to incite Maya's anger more.

"You are nothing but a magnet for men," she said with a glare on her face.

"Maya, really what's the problem?" I asked.

"Oh, fuck this," she said in clearly a bad mood. The waiter had brought over a chardonnay she must have ordered before my arrival. She took a swig. "I broke up with my girlfriend."

"Oh — I didn't know you had a girlfriend," I said.

"Sí, you never asked," she replied.

I sat back a little in my chair and realized she was just resentful. I picked up a sugar packet and fiddled with it. "I'm not a very good friend. I'm sorry. What happened with your girlfriend?"

"She knows I love someone else. She dump me," she said frankly.

"You love someone else?" I asked and frowned.

Maya shifted uneasily in her seat and took another drink of chardonnay. "You think you stay with Kale?" she said, suddenly changing the subject.

"Yes," I replied, and as I said it, I realized it felt great to be at ease with my feelings. "We're a great team. He wants to teach me more about production."

"You love him?" she asked.

I didn't want to talk with Maya about how deeply I loved Kale. Her demeanor was unsettling, and she seemed angry with me. I felt like we were somehow on our way to some kind of showdown, and I didn't know why. "You know what? I told Kale I would meet him for a late drink at the house," I said as I stood up. "I'm going to head out. Is that okay?"

Maya stood up too, reached out and hugged me tight. "Sí, you go. I'll be fine."

I nodded, kissed her cheek and headed out of the restaurant. The long walk to my car was a relief. I felt like I had just dodged some kind of confrontation. Kale was not expecting me, so I texted him that I was coming over. He agreed to meet me at the house.

I arrived at his house some time later. Kale was in the living room that overlooked his lavish green yard and pool below. He was drinking some hard liquor that I assumed was scotch and laying length-wise on the sofa with his head resting on the pillow against the armrest. His long arm hung over the edge of the sofa with the drink in his hand. His gentle blue-green eyes shifted over toward me and he smiled. I walked over, slipped off my shoes and slid on top of his long torso – he was such a big guy that he left no room on the edge to really snuggle. He didn't seem to mind my weight on him, and I didn't weigh much anyway. He moved my hair away from my forehead, turned my head toward him and he kissed me long and lingeringly. I tasted the bitter liquor in his mouth and pulled away.

"What are you drinking?" I asked. "It's strong!"

"Scotch, you want some?" he offered.

I reached over, took his glass out of his outstretched hand, took a brief sip and then kissed him. I pulled away and his eyes were closed. He was taking me in. Kale loved to savor moments, which I thought was special about him. He didn't just rush to the next thing. He could linger in a minute, and I could see the enjoyment and gratification written all over his angular but soft-looking expression.

"Can I ask you something?"

Kale opened his eyes, looked at me and nodded. "Sweetheart … "

"When we broke up, was — was it really that bad for you?" I tentatively asked.

Kale studied me for a moment and slowly nodded without saying a word. I stared at him and felt horribly. He could read my every quiver now and pulled my head so he could look me closely in the eyes. "It's part of the package, sweetheart. Get it?"

"Not really," I softly replied.

Kale took another sip and continued to look at me intensely. "If you didn't mean that much, I wouldn't have given you a second chance," he admitted in such an honest, vulnerable way. "Come on, look at me. Do I seem like the type of guy who likes being on your backburner?"

"I'm not used to that," I admitted.

Kale frowned and replied, "That's sad, sweetheart." He grinned. "You are the only woman I ever gave a second chance – and it's worth it," he said and grabbed me by the back of the neck to kiss me long and deep. He then pulled away and looked at me questioningly. "Why are you asking this tonight?"

"I saw Maya," I replied.

"Hmm … well, you let me worry about my feelings. Have you thought about my offer?" he asked.

"Yes," I replied.

"And?" he asked expectantly and waited for my response.

"Don't you think I should get some other credit somewhere else? I mean, well, what if we don't work out? Your career is established. Mine not so much. What would I do?"

"Then I suppose we need to work out," he said and grinned at me.

"Seriously, Kale, unless we get married, which is a long-shot, then what?"

"Maybe it's not a long-shot," he said, just that plainly.

I lurched away and sat straight up. "Whoa! Look, we're not … "

He didn't let me finish that sentence. Instead, he grabbed my entire body and pulled me on him. He grinded his hips into me and kissed me somewhat roughly and passionately. I felt his large hands push my black skirt up and yank my lacy panties off. He began to rub, touch and use his fingers. I moaned in unexpected pleasure. He kept kissing me very passionately and hungrily. With his other hand, he pushed up my top and moved under my bra so he could fondle my breasts. I felt his tongue in my mouth and he gave me a slight lick. He swiftly rolled me over on the sofa, undid his belt and pulled out his huge, hard cock so he could replace his finger with it. I was so caught up in the surprise of this unexpected tryst that I could hardly react. He was kissing and fucking me relentlessly. I was so turned on the lust was building up. I gripped his back and dug my fingers into his skin as the tension built. I was surprised as I heard his breath catch and he moaned and released. I was right there with him – and off I went with a rush of excitement, delight and relief. My thighs quivered and quaked with tremors as multiple orgasms rolled through my body.

I rested beneath him and felt his warmth and sweat. Beads of sweat covered his forehead. I raised my hand and gently swiped it off into his damp, fine hair. He looked exhausted and satisfied all at once. I realized he had used sex to divert the confrontation and serious discussion that obviously wasn't in his favor. He looked down at me and didn't move off me like he would normally have done. He wrapped one arm around my small waist and rolled me back on top of him. He rested one arm behind his head and he looked at me with a relaxed beam of satisfaction.

"Is it really humanly possible to have this much great sex with one person?" I asked suddenly.

Kale looked down his nose at me and chuckled. "It would seem so," he replied and sighed.

"You know lust doesn't last," I said.

Kale nodded, smiled, closed his eyes and replied, "This isn't just lust, now is it, sweetheart?"

"What happens when you tire of me? Then will you find a younger version and toss me back like one of those, what did you call them? Oh yeah, 'trash fish.'"

Kale laughed and shook his head. "One minute she screams at the possibility of a real commitment and the next compares herself to a shitty fish? Are you serious?"

"Maybe," I wryly replied.

"Well, don't be," he said as he opened one eye to look at me. "Now bring me those lips and that body and let's go upstairs and make love some more."

I laughed, moved up his chest and kissed him. I then pulled away and said, "Okay. If you're addicted, you won't be able to throw me back."

He hungrily kissed me and replied, "Who would want to?"

Chapter 23

We decided to go to Kale's Santa Barbara compound. When he said compound, I immediately wondered how big this little seaside shack might be. I knew Kale had money – lots of money – but we really didn't talk about that sort of thing. I thought it was great that he was so successful, but my interest in him actually had little to do with his bank accounts. We were, at this point, both focused on our respective careers. Our common bond came from a shared interest in filmmaking and a similar aesthetic toward art and life. I honestly didn't think Kale cared that much about money other than seeing it as a means to an end and as a way to enjoy his freedom. Even all of his material things were just fun distractions for him. And, like I said, we just didn't talk about it. Every time he surprised me with things like an invitation to a previously unmentioned "compound" in Santa Barbara, I never asked questions, which inevitably led to clueless surprises when boats turned into yachts complete with deckhands.

I brought my MacBook Air to work poolside. Kale quickly reminded me this trip was for relaxation and not work. I was loading my bags into the back of his Mercedes when he saw the suspect laptop case.

"Sweetheart, no work." He gave me a look of disapproval.

He started to reach into my black bag to pull out the hot-pink-and-black-checkered case. I pulled it away from his grasp. "Uh-uh, I find writing relaxing," I asserted.

Kale shook his head. "Fine, but only if I get to see the new script," he replied as he attempted to negotiate an agreement.

I was wearing flat, black flip-flops with a fuchsia-colored knit dress so I had to stand on my tiptoes to reach his mouth to kiss him. "We'll see about that, Mr. Producer," I said as I dropped back down to my flat feet.

Kale put the last bag in the trunk, nodded at me and then went and opened my car door. I dropped into the convertible and waited for him to get in. Kale's phone rang just as we pulled out. He grabbed his Bluetooth, shoved it in his ear and pressed the button to answer.

"Yeah," he said and listened. "Okay, all right sounds good. See you tonight," he said and turned to me with a look on his face. "Did you tell Ryan where we were going?"

"He called earlier. Why?" I asked.

"Because he and his daddy are in Santa Barbara and want to have drinks with us tonight."

"Huh? Why?" I asked.

"Some project he wants to discuss," said Kale with a shrug.

"And you let them interrupt our weekend?" I asked protectively.

"Hmm ... it will be interesting. Ry-Ry's daddy owns a piece of every major distributor in the U.S. and U.K. He can make my life really difficult," cautioned Kale. "So we'll take drinks with him and see what he has in mind."

About an hour later, we pulled up to a tall iron-rod security gate. Kale pressed a button and the gates swung open to reveal a Tuscan-style mansion with a turret in the center and glass windows with full views toward the Pacific Ocean. The front of the house was made with red bricks and crumbling cement that looked like it was decaying. In front of the windows were rows of colorful wild flowers and small bushes short enough to not block the windows. As I always did, I masked my expression of awe. One thing you could say about Kale: He had amazing taste and style. The house, while at least two stories high, was not garish or large. It was elegant and chic much like his Beverly Hills house. A semicircular driveway allowed Kale to pull the car up close to the front door so we could easily unload the bags.

As he politely unloaded our bags, I got out of the car and took it all in. Cyprus and palm trees grew along the edges of the property. I could hear seagulls squawking off in the distance. Kale reached into his pants pocket, pulled out the house keys, unlocked the front door and swung it open so I could walk in. As I entered, the house smelled like it had been closed up for some time. It felt and smelled warm and dusty but not in a bad way. Kale immediately flipped on the thermostat to cool things down. In front of me, a small stairwell dropped forward, so that as I walked down I was at hill level and facing the great picture windows that looked out onto the vast, reaching blue of the ocean. It was a stunning view. Another stairwell off to the right led to a door that went outside to a patio where I could see wooden patio furniture and the glimmer of a swimming pool. Kale disappeared, I assumed to put away our bags, and I just stood at the top of the stairs, gazing at the incredible view. I felt appreciative and spoiled all at once. I slowly walked down without taking my gaze off the ocean. It made me feel relaxed.

Kale soon emerged from the back somewhere, and he had a glass of pink champagne in his hand. He came up behind me, wrapped one arm around my waist and handed me the glass.

"Oh, thank you," I said as I took the glass and sipped it from the top.

Just as I said that, Mat Kearney's album *City of Black and White* came on over the speakers built into the ceiling. The first song "All I Have" played over the speakers. Kale grabbed me gently by my lower back and pulled me into him so we were dancing and hugging. I took another sip and set down my glass and then I fully wrapped myself around him to hug him. I heard him say "hmm" quietly like he was savoring the touch of my body against his. Like I said, he was the kind of guy who took in the moment and owned every piece of it. I felt like a comforting blanket to him – it wasn't sexual I could tell. He seemed to be taking in my presence, energy and affection and enjoying it. I was his drug of choice – his aphrodisiac and elixir. I looked up at him – his eyes were closed and he looked absolutely serene. His face glowed in all its rugged radiance. This prompted me to stand on my tiptoes and give him a long and sensual kiss. I lowered my body back down and continued to hug him as the next song came on called "Fire and Rain." We were swaying back and forth entangled in each other.

I looked back up at him and said, "You are beautiful."

Kale opened his eyes, smiled and replied, "Aren't I supposed to say that to you, sweetheart?"

"You can if you want," I said with a laugh.

Kale nodded and smiled. "Well, you are," he said as he guided me to sit down on the sofa so we could take in the view together.

He suddenly reached into his pocket and pulled out his iPhone and said, "I should text Maya to come down and cook for us since we're having guests tonight."

As Kale said this, he picked up his phone and quickly texted something. I figured the mission was accomplished because he set the phone back down almost immediately. A small part of me felt really guilty having someone else come and cook. This luxury wasn't something I was used to or felt privileged enough to ask someone to do. I was accustomed to doing my own cooking and cleaning for that matter.

Kale, who now knew me so well, frowned and nudged me and then what he said surprised me: "She's not your equal."

"What?" I said.

"Brea, it's not a class thing. You shouldn't feel weird about it. I know you're friends, but it's her job."

"I know," I replied quietly.

"You're such a considerate person, and I know you're not used to this," he said and looked around. "But I like that about you, too. You're not all jaded and fucked up ... yet," he remarked with a chuckle. “I give you two more years.”

I started laughing. “Really? Only two? I say one – especially with people like Curtis around.”

“Ah, there’s that sense of humor.” He smiled, leaned over and kissed me. “Curtis can’t do anything. I took care of him.”

“How so?”

“Ah, let’s not talk about that right now,” he said and grinned. “I have a better idea.”

He gently pushed my shoulders back so that I was on my back. I laughed and said, “Of course you do.”

He looked at me and slowly crawled on top of me. “You haven’t seen the bedroom yet,” he suddenly said and then got up, extended his hand to help me and pulled me up. We walked up the stairs and off to the left toward the end of the hallway. He pushed open two glass doors to reveal a huge contemporary four-poster bed positioned in front of a floor-to-ceiling picture window facing the ocean. The evening light shone through the windows to cast a pale yellow glow over the room that was carpeted in all white and decorated with Tuscan-style furniture. The very top of the four-poster bed was connected with a canopy that looked like tree branches reaching across. Kale smiled at my expression and slinked in behind me with a cocky kind of strut. He rarely seemed proud of something – but this brought him some kind of strange male pride. He moved ahead of me, grabbed my hands, lowered himself onto the bed’s end and then pulled me down on top of him so we were kissing. The kissing slowly heated up, and he picked me up with a sudden pull and playfully threw me further onto the bed. I laughed as he turned and seemed to prowl up to me, keeping his eyes fixed on me. I gulped a little. He looked almost scary like he was about to devour me like prey.

He got this intense look on his face, raised one eyebrow and said, "What do you want little girl?"

I grinned and smiled. "You."

"Say it again," he said as he continued to stare me down with that lustful look.

"You," I obliged.

"Really? How much?" he asked.

I crawled forward and climbed up him like some jungle gym, lifted his shirt so I could run my hands on his muscular stomach and then gave him a seductive look. "Who's the bitch?" I asked with my own sinister look.

"You want me to say that?" he gasped a little and asked with that same serious look.

I let me fingers crawl down his stomach just a little bit and stopped just a few inches from the top of his pants. "Yes," I responded simply.

Kale shook his head. "Uh-uh, I'm nobody's bitch – not even yours."

I suddenly thrust my hand down into his pants, and I clutched him. I saw his eyes glaze a bit as he tried to maintain some semblance of control. "Are you sure?" I asked with a sexy smirk.

Kale didn't flinch. He had amazing control and continued to look me in the eyes. "Positive," he said and ever so gently touched the top of my head and lightly pushed me down toward him. For the sake of letting him maintain his alpha posture, I laughed a little bit, shrugged and said, "I guess I am."

Kale reached around and slapped my ass. "Yes, you are."

I undid his top button and unzipped his fly. Then I artfully yanked his pants down, looked at him with a devilish grin and went for it. The minute my tongue touched him, he breathed heavily and became intensely focused on my actions. I kissed and sucked him. He moaned and loved my attention. I kissed all the way around him and then made my way back up his torso, kissing him along the way. He then stripped my clothes off and threw each piece across the room. Once I was naked, I nodded at him to signal his turn. He stripped too. He stood there and stared at me, and when I least expected it, he grabbed me by the waist and pulled me against him so that I was on my knees and he was still standing. The minute our naked bodies touched, it felt hot. He pulled me by the back of the neck, ran his hands through my hair, rubbed my neck and pushed me into a hot kiss. He pushed me back so I was flat on my back in front of him. He reached over, grabbed some kind of remote and hit a button – the windows were on tracks and slid back into the walls. I could hear the waves below rhythmically crashing. I sat up on my elbows to look outside and felt a cool breeze blow in. I was completely amazed.

Kale looked over his shoulder for a moment. "It's a great view – but this one is better," he said as his eyes rested on my naked body.

He slowly moved completely on top of me. He looked me right in the eyes, kissed me gently once, smiled and said, "Love you, sweetheart."

His eyes sparkled when he said that. My heart melted. This hot man was completely amazing and communicated with his facial expressions that showed every emotion without a single word. He moved me. Yes, that was the exact phrase that went through my mind. I studied his kind, chiseled face and felt infinitely connected to his emotional world right then. What we had together was comfortable and calm. I felt like I had come home to his embrace and love. Isn't that all a girl can hope for? Love and forgiveness – he had given me those two gifts. Right then, I knew the whole Drew mess was truly over and behind us. Maybe it was the test of our relationship. Maybe it was our Velveteen Rabbit moment and now we would be real. In that one indefinable moment, I didn't see my future with someone else. All the questions were gone. I was in all the way – and I was in very deep.

"You are the love of my life," I admitted completely and freely. All my fear was gone. I could say that and trust him. He wasn't going to use it against me or run away.

Kale rolled off to the side, blinked for a moment and just stared at me. His lust had quieted into an emotional reaction. He had been physically moved. Now he was utterly still before reaching out and softly running his finger along the edge of my cheek. He warmly smiled as he said, "Then marry me!"

Now I was in shock. My mouth dropped open, and I said, "What?"

"Don't say, 'what,' just say 'yes,'" he replied and smiled gently.

I looked up at the ceiling. A warm, comforting feeling flowed through me. I turned back to find his eyes fixed on me. He still looked serene. I knew why. Because he knew like I did that there could be no other answer. I nodded and whispered, "Yes."

He smiled, pulled me up on top of him and then moved up so he could kiss me. We then made love for the next hour until we knew Maya would show up. And it was a whole new sexual encounter infused with nothing but tenderness. What a difference a day makes, I thought as I settled against him to nap.

Chapter 24

Maya arrived first with a bag in hand. It was too far to drive back after dinner. Kale put her bag in the guest room on the first floor below the kitchen. She immediately went to the kitchen to begin cooking. She hardly looked my way when she walked in. I was sitting at the center counter, drinking champagne and munching on green grapes out of a brown porcelain bowl. Kale strolled into the kitchen and immediately came up behind me, moved my hair back to kiss my neck and then rested his arms around me, leaning on the counter for support. I glanced back at him. He looked rosy, flush and contented. His lips were a soft pink to match his cheeks.

"Why don't you hang here with Maya when Burt arrives, so that we can get the business stuff out of the way first, and then come down when dinner is ready?" he suggested softly, almost in a whisper. I had never heard Ryan's father's name before so I assumed he was Burt.

I turned just a bit and kissed him on the lips. I smiled up at him and nodded. "Sure, no problem."

Kale looked me in the eyes with a twinge of lust. He sighed. "This is not how I planned to spend this evening," he complained.

Maya heard that comment and looked at us. I could tell she wanted to say something but held back. Kale noticed too and said, "Hey, you make sure you join us for dinner. Don't just serve the food, all right?"

Maya looked at him – and they shared a connected stare. It was so evident how much Kale respected her not just as a housekeeper but also as a friend. I could see a reluctance in Maya's expression, but also I realized she would agree despite any reticence, just to please him. She quietly nodded as she looked down and began breaking green beans apart. As I watched her hands move, I felt Kale's hand slide up the back of my top to rub my back and then move up and under my breasts where I felt his fingertips probe. It made me very hot and horny. I rotated around on the barstool so our eyes could meet. I gave him a look. He smiled and laughed a little – he got it.

"Unless we have time to make good on that promise, please don't do that," I quietly whispered.

My eyes also shifted down and he was just as aroused. He stood there a moment and shrugged. "All right," he said and acquiesced. "We could go up … " he started to say when I just shook my head at him.

"No, but tonight," I reassured him and kept my voice very low.

"A good reason to get this meeting over with," he said just as the doorbell rang. "Ah, perfect," he said, kissed my forehead and glided off to answer the door.

I heard a lot of noise, and Ryan's boisterous voice as he said "hey, man" really loudly. Within seconds Ryan flew into the room, grabbed me and hugged me, and then nodded at Maya. Then he turned to expose his father – a lean, muscular older man with salt-and-pepper hair and a neatly trimmed short gray beard who wore a V-collar black sweater and slate-gray pants. He looked chic and comfortable and very metrosexual. Ryan was his dad's spitting image only with sandy blonde hair and slightly taller. When Burt saw me, his eyes lit up, and his pupils dilated to indicate he was attracted to me, which made me incredibly uncomfortable. He didn't shake my hand but rather kissed it, which made me want to recoil from him.

"The gorgeous Brea Harper," he said with a leering smile.

Ryan was popping grapes into his mouth and hardly noticed his father's gesture. He also had already grabbed the champagne bottle and poured himself a drink. He was distracted and looking around without catching his father's advances while Kale, on the other hand, looked from Burt to me and stepped forward in a protective move. He immediately put his arm around my waist and pulled me in close.

"Brea agreed to marry me today," Kale suddenly announced to my shock. I didn't realize we were going to openly tell people; but also I sensed he revealed our intentions to let Burt know I was spoken for. The minute he uttered those words, Ryan quit acting like an ADD-inflicted schoolboy and stared with his mouth gaped open like a hooked fish; Maya just stopped chopping mid-chop to stare at us.

"Congratulations," offered Burt who shook Kale's hand.

Ryan and Maya stood back in silence.

"Thank you, sir," said Kale politely as he continued to grip me like some pitbull with its jaw locked on a favorite toy.

Not unlike Ryan and Maya, I was silent too.

"Isn't this your second engagement?" blurted Ryan. "You were with that actress chick weren't you … what was her name? Sherry something?"

Kale turned toward Ryan and replied, "Yes, Cheryl."

Ah yes, Cheryl, the woman who once threw her engagement ring at me. I had never heard her actual name before. I had never asked either. Kale looked nervously at me, but when I gave him no discernable stress, he smiled and said, "Do you mind, sweetheart? Burt and I are going to retire to the patio, aren't we, Burt?"

I nodded; Kale sweetly kissed me and led Burt out to the patio.

Ryan, who could now safely move in close, shook his head at me. "Really?" he asked. "You're going to marry that dickhead?"

"He's not a dickhead," spat Maya. "And when did you quit fucking the men to get engaged?" she angrily yelled at me.

I looked at them both. "Way to go guys. Love the support."

"Weren't you just fucking me a few weeks ago?" asked Ryan. "Jesus, you move fast."

"It's not like that," I retorted and felt defensive. "Christ, both of you just fuck off," I said in a raised voice and headed downstairs to the living room to sit.

I was sitting alone and turned to where I could see Kale

and Burt talking at the patio table. Kale's expressive eyes were worried – I could see it. He appeared to be listening intently and not talking when Ryan bounded into the room and planted himself next to me on the sofa. He kind of playfully leaned over to me and put his head down on my lap to catch my gaze. I looked down at him and laughed at his way of getting my attention.

"We should fuck this juke joint, get wasted and fuck all night."

"No," I said simply.

Ryan chuckled in amusement. "All right, have it your way, Burger Queen."

"Why do you think Kale's a dickhead?" I asked suddenly.

Ryan shrugged, looked down to pick at his thumbnail and then just rolled his eyes. "He's too fucking old for you, babe. He's like what, 40?"

"No, 35," I replied. "Age doesn't matter."

"You're deluded darling," he said. "The man wants to build a fucking nest and put some baby birds in it. You want that? I don't think so."

Ryan's words resonated. I didn't want any baby birds or a nest for that matter, but I didn't want to lose Kale either. I felt at home with him, and he wanted the security of commitment. It's also not like we had set a date or anything. Maybe we could be one of those couples who were engaged forever. And I did want Kale to feel secure and know I felt just as seriously. Ryan wasn't looking at me anymore. He was drinking heavily. I was glad his dad drove. I glanced back over at Kale and Burt. Now

I could see Kale talking very seriously. His expression was stern – and that alarmed me. Something uncomfortable was clearly going down outside. I wanted to go to him, but I knew Kale would be angry if I showed up so I sat still.

I told Ryan I needed to help Maya and slipped back up to the kitchen. Ryan was still drinking on the sofa. Maya only briefly looked up at me and didn't say anything. She was now at the stove and sautéing vegetables in a wok. She was an amazing cook and the smell of the spices wafted in the air all around us. She was acting strangely and not making eye contact with me.

"Hey, you know, I do love Kale," I assured. "And weren't you the one who encouraged me to make him my Mr. Harper?"

Maya was vigorously stirring some sauce and barely glanced up at me. "You don't need to explain to me," she said abruptly. "I'm Mr. Kale's maid. I have no right to judge or interfere."

"Maya, I thought we were friends," I argued. "I don't like that you're mad at me. Kale and I worked it all out. Please just be happy for us."

Maya stopped stirring for a moment, looked up, gave me a strange look and said, "What I'm happy about doesn't matter."

Just then Ryan walked into the kitchen and sat down. He stumbled a little, and he was totally tanked. He looked up at me with drunken eyes and started laughing. "You sure you want this Kale dude?"

I threw up my arms and said, "You're both crazy," and I turned and went back down to the living room to escape both of them. Just as I walked downstairs, the patio door opened, and Burt stormed in clearly angry with a sullen Kale right behind him.

Burt looked right at me and smiled this strange way and then yelled, "Ryan! We're leaving."

Ryan stumbled out of the kitchen. Burt took one look at him, rolled his eyes, and grabbed him by the shoulders and pushed him toward the front door. Then he turned back to me, extended his hand and said, "Brea, so nice meeting you. And I'll be in touch."

Just as he shook my hand, Kale came up behind me and folded his arms against his chest. Kale only vaguely nodded as Burt exited. I turned toward him concerned and asked, "What was that all about?"

Kale looked down at me, arched one eyebrow, and then turned and walked up into the kitchen.

"That's not an answer," I called after him. I then raced upstairs right on his heels. "What the fuck is going on?" I demanded.

Kale looked at Maya and said, "When is dinner going to be served?"

Maya glanced up and replied, "Ten minutes."

Kale nodded and shifted his eyes away from her and then took off for the master suite. I tailed behind him, feeling very anxious about all of this. Kale was typically forthright, and he was obviously holding back for a reason, which scared me.

Kale walked straight into the bedroom with me close behind. As soon as I walked through the door, he grabbed me, slammed the door and pushed me onto the bed. He began tearing off my clothes and kissing me very hard and passionately. I was both alarmed and turned on. He stripped off his clothes just as quickly and pushed me back onto to the bed. He moved right on top of me swiftly and gracefully and we were making love before I could think straight. He buried his face in my neck, kissing me all over and down to my breasts as he thrust into me over and over. His hands were all over me, touching and stroking and moving. My head was swirling, and I was completely lost in lust. He was like that Dave Matthews' song "Crash into Me," and we were on this intense, sexual collision of bodies, heat and sweat. I could barely breathe.

Before I could even react, he was touching me rhythmically and working very hard to pleasure me. I gasped and opened my eyes in total shock and desire. I could barely move or react. The pressure was building up faster than I could think and my body was nothing but a pure reaction to touch. I started gripping Kale's muscular biceps and felt afraid my grip would hurt him it was so tight. My mouth opened almost like I could scream; I sucked in air and then it hit in orgasmic waves of pure ecstasy. I came harder than I've ever experienced as multiple orgasms just went on and on. Kale looked down at me with such a pleased smile and then he focused on his own needs, and he released and came right after me.

He fell back onto the bed next to me, breathing heavily. I turned my head and looked over at his sweaty body. He glistened in all his muscular exquisiteness. I was also out of breath and closed my eyes for a moment. He suddenly got up and off the bed completely naked and walked outside. I raised my head and felt worried again. His reaction was very un-Kale like in behavior. He was actually putting physical space between us, which he never did after our lovemaking. He loved to hold me close. Now I was even more alarmed and slid off the bed to stand next to him.

"Tell me," I said quietly as I touched his muscular upper arm where I had left red marks from my grip.

Kale looked at me sadly, nodded and said, "Burt is threatening to pull distribution for your film if I don't give you to his studio."

"What? He can do that? What if I don't want to work for him?"

Kale looked off over the ocean with such a heavy look of worry. He was quiet and then when he spoke, he didn't look at me. "I have millions of dollar vested here, Brea. You have to."

I reeled from that answer. I felt my mind and body separate. He was betraying me! He was selling me out! He was putting money and the film ahead of me – ahead of us. I turned and retreated to a brown leather chair in the corner of the room. Kale turned and followed me in. He got on his knees in front of me.

"Don't do this, sweetheart," he begged. "We're a team. Take one for the team."

"Team? You sold me out, Kale! You sold me out!" I repeated

in complete shock. "How could you do that?"

Kale looked completely bereaved and upset, too. "No, no don't say that. I didn't."

I looked him right in the eye. "But you did!" I protested. "Why does he want me so badly anyway? I'm not that talented!"

Kale looked completely sad and could barely look at me. "You are that talented, sweetheart. You just don't know it."

"That's not it, Kale! That's not it! Tell me the truth!" I cried out.

Kale stared at me long and hard and then quietly whispered, "It is."

"No, it's not!" I replied. "I know it's not. Turn over a rock, find a writer," I said and looked away. I was so lost. I didn't know what to do or say. My talent wasn't the answer. The truth, why wouldn't he tell me? I could see it in his eyes he wanted to. And there we were – both stark naked emotionally and physically. I felt suddenly sick to my stomach.

I slid down in the chair so that my knees came to rest on Kale's bare chest. "It's not," I repeated again. "And I don't feel so good."

Kale grabbed me and gently pulled me forward like a child against a parent so he could comfort me. "It is," he quietly repeated. "Please believe me. I'm so fucking sorry for this."

"How can I lose control over my life like this?" I asked as a heavy sadness rolled a fog over my mind. "I want to lie down."

I moved away from Kale, pulled back the comforter on the

bed and slid under it. Kale stood up and just looked at me. I threw the comforter over my head. "Go away," I cried for him to leave.

Kale moved over closer; I could feel his heat. "I'll leave you for now, but you're not shutting me out. Come down for dinner when it's ready."

Then I heard some shuffling and the door opened and closed. I lay there under that comforter. I used the blanket like a shield from the world. How could this have happened? How could this stranger make these kinds of demands? How could Kale sell me out so quickly? How could I go from being the happiest woman in the world to this? And all this "fucked-up-ness" happened within hours? I closed my eyes.

Chapter 25

It was Maya who came in and woke me up. I looked at the clock. I had fallen completely asleep and it was 8:00 p.m. – way past dinnertime. She told me she had held dinner and that Kale was waiting for me out on the patio. I put on a blue slip dress and headed downstairs. I felt groggy. Had it been a dream? No, it was real. As I opened the patio door, I saw candles glowing all around the table's base and on the table itself. I looked over – and there was Kale sitting on one end bathed in candle light, which made him look way too elegant for a man. He stood up and extended his hand for me to walk over. Coldplay's "We Never Change" was playing through the speakers. He pulled the chair back so I could sit down, which I did, and he scooted the chair back in for me.

"Sweetheart, I didn't want to wake you; you must have been tired," he said.

I nodded and didn't say a word. How could he act like nothing had happened? The meal consisted of filet mignon with button mushrooms and a brown sauce, sautéed vegetables and a small heap of summer fruit. I cut a piece of meat and savored it. Maya, true to form, had outdone herself. We didn't talk for a bit as we each quietly ate and listened to the music. OneRepublic's "The Good Life" was playing. Yes, it was a good life until someone told you in not so many words that you were nothing more than chattel to be bought and sold. I had become a commodity. I knew I had the power to say no to all of this, but then I would hurt Kale. I would destroy our relationship, and I would probably be out of a job altogether. What would rebelling against the situation accomplish?

"Aren't there any alternative distributors you could use?" I suddenly asked.

Kale looked up and realized he wasn't going to avoid more of this conversation. "Burt will blackball it across the board, sweetheart. The business side is very complicated. All it takes is something like this to destroy a project before it even gets out of the gate."

"I just don't get it," I said quietly. "Why me? Why this?"

"Burt has an agenda, and you're a part of it," said Kale. "Burt and I go way back. He's fucked with my projects in the past."

"Why, though?"

Kale looked down. "I dated his daughter, and we broke up."

My mouth dropped. "Ryan never mentioned a sister. Why did you break up?"

"She's his stepsister – and does it matter?" he said.

I stared at him and said, "Yes, it does. Because here we are."

Kale stiffened, and I could tell he didn't want to tell me. I waited. Instead, he just continued to eat and look at me for a minute. "I'm not going to tell you," he suddenly replied. "Now, please back off," he snapped in a very uncharacteristic way.

The tone he took chastened me and reminded me of an earlier time when I got caught with Drew and how Kale reacted in his office by being dismissive of me. I looked down and allowed my head to droop a bit. I was completely reeling and upset – there were too many unexpected and offensive things going on between us. I felt angry, too. He had no right to be mad at me. I wasn't the one who obviously had done something in my past to screw up my future. My perfect man was getting more chinks in his shining armor.

He could see the mixed feelings on my face. He reached across the table and touched my hand. "This isn't about you," he said flatly.

"How can you say that? It clearly involves me," I replied.

"Please let's not ruin this weekend," he pleaded. "I just want to be alone with you, all right?"

I shrugged and considered it. I didn't really want to spend the entire weekend in a fight. I also didn't want to face the truth – that I could be forced to work for some jerk with a hidden agenda. And then I decided to do what I did best – ignore the problem. I finished my meal and sat back in my chair. I studied Kale's face lit by the candlelight. He looked so magnificent. Okay, so I would use his beautiful form as a sexy distraction. His blonde hair looked dark in this light, and his eyes reflected the candle flames so that they sparkled.

Once he finished eating, he sat back in his chair and looked right at me. He didn't seem as agitated now. Maya brought out some port wine for dessert, which I slowly sipped. After a few moments, the alcohol got into my system, and I started to relax for the first time that evening. I wanted to forget about what had happened, but despite my best efforts, I was having trouble quieting my mind.

Kale slid his chair closer to mine so he could kiss me. I responded and decided that for now, I needed to focus only on him. I stared into his eyes and noticed his day-old stubble was getting thicker. I reached out and touched his rough cheek and lightly ran my fingertips through the stubble. He was so masculine and easy on the eyes. He laughed a little at the gesture.

"You feeling better?" he asked suddenly.

"Not really," I replied, determined not to make a bad situation somehow easier for him. I inwardly hoped he would figure out another alternative to the problem. "But I don't want to argue about it anymore."

"Well good," he replied and then suddenly sat back a little and took a sip of port. "Besides, maybe Burt will back off."

I didn't reply but instead got up and moved over to him. He slid his chair back to open his lap up for me. I straddled him with my legs on each side so I could face him. He sat back a little and just admired me for a moment – he had this very self-satisfied look on his face.

"Ryan wanted to fuck you again, didn't he?" Kale asked rather abruptly as he pushed my hair back onto my shoulders so he could see into my eyes.

I nodded slowly and answered, "Yes, and so do you."

Kale lowered his face onto my chest to kiss and lick me down to my breast. He then looked up at me. "Every single day, sweetheart."

His mouth and tongue then found their way down to the edge of my black bra. He reached up and pushed my top down, followed by my bra straps so that my breasts were exposed to his tease. He continued to kiss and gently lick just a little bit. His tongue found my nipples, and he bit just slightly which made me sit up in surprise and excitement.

"Did he ask you to?" Kale continued this line of questioning all the while kissing, sucking and enjoying my breasts.

"Yes," I answered again.

"Did you want him?"

"Why, do you want to watch?" I asked just to be sexy, but I felt Kale react to that and stiffen a bit.

Kale grabbed me by the neck and moved my head so I was looking right at him. "Do you want me to?"

Now I was surprised and a little uncertain about what he wanted to hear. Was this a test? Did he really want to watch me with another man? He looked pretty serious about this question. His eyes rested on mine without so much as a blink. I pondered what to say, but then he was still breathing heavily and not at all turned off. The only answer seemed to be sexual, so that was where I went – and maybe down a forbidden path.

"Yes," I whispered.

Oh, and this set Kale off into frenzy of pure lust. The light kissing turned much fiercer and passionate. He immediately undid his pants and let his huge cock out. He then abruptly pulled off my underwear, flung them away from us, lifted me up and rested me on top of him. I panted in ecstasy and pulled my legs up so I was propping them on the edge of the chair to get the sexiest position. Kale's eyes widened in excitement as he watched me move. I began working him intensely, and he gripped the back of my neck with his fingers tangled in my blonde hair. His eyes fluttered a bit as he tried not to lose it. I kept working him a little harder. His head threw back and then he leveled his gaze at me.

"God, you're fucking beautiful," he cried out, and I could tell it was all he could do to hold back.

He reached down and began pleasuring me as he kissed my lips. His tongue played with mine. I was now feeling the thrill build up. I kept going at him. He continued to kiss me, and then he threw his head back and couldn't take it any longer. He cried in a soft moan, which just set me off. We literally came at the same time, each of us completely lost in our own gratification. I felt the quake of orgasm and then my head fell forward onto his chest as my thighs quivered. I finally had a moment to think. Did he really want to see me with Ryan? Now my head was swimming with a whole slew of new questions. Why did he ask me that? Was there so much more to this story than I already knew about? Maybe Ryan would tell me. I decided I would have to question Ryan when I got home.

Chapter 26

The next day we woke up bright and early. The discussion of the night before had dissolved into a blissful night of love-making and no more talking. I think we both felt like there was nothing more to talk about until things got sorted out. Kale wanted to go to a winery called Wine Cask for brunch. He said it was gorgeous and told Maya not to make breakfast. He also invited Maya to join us, and she seemed to soften and agreed to come along.

Maya and I were dressed and waiting in the kitchen. I was sitting at a barstool in a cream-colored flowing skirt and black sleeveless top with a wide black belt, and Maya was leaning on the counter reading a book in Spanish. She said it was still easier for her to read in Spanish than English. Kale came gliding into the room. He looked rugged and handsome in his abused-looking but chic jeans and button-down, khaki-colored shirt over the top of a slate-colored T-shirt. He moved straight behind me, touched my waist, leaned in and kissed my neck.

"Hmm … you smell good, sweetheart," he whispered. "Hey, can you do me a quick favor and send the latest script to Erin for me?" he asked in a louder voice.

"Oh, my battery died, and I forgot the charger," I replied. "Maya, did you bring a laptop?"

Maya glanced up from her reading and hardly seemed to notice and just nodded. She kept right on reading.

"I can access my Gmail account and pull the last draft from my inbox and send it," I offered.

"Great, could you do that while I grab my wallet?" asked Kale.

I nodded and headed off to Maya's room downstairs on the ground floor. I trotted very cheerfully into the only bedroom where Maya had already neatly made the bed. The sun shone through a ground-level window and created a warm light on the beige comforter. I looked around and spotted Maya's bags in the corner and what clearly looked like a laptop case. I took out the AirBook and leaned on the bed to open the lid. I was scanning the desktop for the Firefox icon when a strange video clip labeled "BandK" caught my attention. I don't know why, but I double-clicked on it, waited a second and then a very unsettling moaning came over the audio and the picture revealed a tight close-up of two people having sex. My eyes widened as I realized the close-up was first of my breasts and then Kale's face emerged as the picture pulled back a little.

I looked up terribly confused, and that's when I saw Maya slowly enter the room. Her eyes looked fearful and her mouth was quivering. I slammed the lid shut and calmly put the laptop back. I was gripped in a self-directed numbness. I stared at her – and our eyes locked in a mental showdown for only a moment. I regained my composure and walked up to her and just stared. My mind flashed back to the night after my first encounter with Kale when she had "joked" about the security cameras and the potential sex tape, which I had questioned her about then. She had firmly denied its existence. Now I knew it was no joke.

"Wait! Chica, I explain!" she said in a fearful, nervous voice.

She went to grab my arm, and I wrenched it away. I shook my head and rushed upstairs. She followed right behind me, trying to grab my arm. I steadied myself and pulled away from her. Now I was broiling in hot anger and rage. I felt beyond violated. Just as I emerged from the top of the stairs, I smacked right into Kale, who immediately saw something terrible was unfolding. He stood erect and looked from me to Maya, who was now desperate and tearful.

Kale looked visibly alarmed. "What's going on?" he asked.

I searched my mind for how to reveal this to him. Every single phrase I could find just didn't soften the blow. I sucked in air and was ready to tell him when Maya started sobbing outright.

"Lo siento, lo siento," she cried. "Por favor." Her Spanish had taken over her for her shaky English.

I turned slightly, looked at her and shook my head. "You're the stalker, aren't you?" I blurted as the reality came rushing to me.

"Lo siento! Lo siento" is all she could say. "Te amo!" she sputtered her confession of love through tears – and it wasn't toward Kale.

I was hit with a thunderous realization she didn't mean as friends. I moved as quickly and reflexively under the protection of Kale who pulled me very close. We both stared at her. She had completely dissolved into a fit of tears at the head of the stairwell. Kale protectively pushed me behind him and stepped forward. He was equally strong and tender with her all at once as they both began speaking in Spanish. I didn't know Kale was fluent in Spanish. He was talking in a stern, but loving manner as he leaned over to talk directly to her. They went back and forth for a minute or so. I had no idea what was being said. Maya managed to compose herself enough and disappeared back downstairs. Kale turned back to me and grabbed my elbow so he could guide me outside and out of earshot.

He opened the front door, helped me out and then stepped into the light. "What did you see, sweetheart?" he asked with concern.

"She's been filming us, Kale," I blurted. "She's the stalker, I know it."

Kale's eyes grew big as he absorbed this news. He steadied himself a bit, realizing the gravity of the situation. He stood up and became very quiet. "She's leaving right now. I'll fire her privately."

I stood back a little. "That's it? Just fire her? What about the files? What else does she have?" I asked, very upset now.

Kale closed his mouth and blinked – I could tell he was just as thrown by this information. "Don't worry, don't … I'll take care of it, sweetheart. I promise. I'll make sure I go through her laptop before she leaves."

"Shouldn't we call the police?" I asked.

Kale kept looking up and down. He was now pensive and nervous. "I — I don't know. I need to talk to her alone. All right? Is that okay? I'll drive her back in her car," he said and reached in his pants pocket. "You take the Mercedes. I'll meet you at your apartment later. Okay?"

I looked down at his keys, took them and tentatively looked back up. "I guess," I said quietly.

"You go now, okay?" he said. "I'll call you."

I slowly nodded. "My purse … "

Kale rushed inside, grabbed my purse from near the doorway where I had left it and handed it to me. "I'll pack you up. All right? Okay?"

I looked up helplessly at him. He was so distressed; it showed in his glassy blue-green eyes. He looked horribly anxious, and I felt just as confused. He looked back at the house and then at me. He saw how unnerved I felt, and he grabbed me and hugged me tightly. He then pulled away, kissed me gently and nodded.

"Okay," he said, calmer now.

I nodded and walked to the Mercedes. Under any other circumstances, I would have been thrilled to drive his convertible home, but not like this. I got in, settled, turned the key, put it in drive and eased the gas pedal. I glanced through the rearview mirror to watch my hot, tall man disappear into the house. Should I leave him alone with her? I felt suddenly scared. Was she crazy? How had I missed crazy? How had Kale? I drove off frightened, anxious and confused. What was next? God! What a shitty weekend!

Chapter 27

I probably should have driven straight home, but my need for answers got the better of me. I found myself driving up into the Hollywood Hills to see Ryan. I hoped he could appeal to his old man and get me out this situation. I pulled up to the gate and hit the speaker button. Ryan's voice came boisterously over the intercom, and he invited me on up. Within minutes, I pulled Kale's car up into Ryan's driveway. I noticed a cute blue convertible Rabbit in the driveway. I wondered about who that could be, and it wasn't long before Ryan came marauding out of the house holding up a pitcher of margaritas with a petite, cute blonde on his back with her legs wrapped around his waist. Ryan was also wearing an oversized sombrero and dancing with the girl hanging from his back like a monkey. Unfamiliar Mexican fiesta music blared from the house and Ryan danced all around me. I couldn't help myself and just started laughing. He was truly crazy and exuberant. He danced around me until the music stopped and switched to the "Macarena," upon which he dropped the blonde off his back and started doing the dance with the pitcher in one hand and his glass in the other.

I stared at him. I couldn't believe this scene happening right in front of me. The little blonde got right behind him and started doing the same thing. Hands up by the head, down at the waist and away they went.

"Come on, Brea," shouted Ryan. "Dance, baby, dance!"

I couldn't help it. I started doing the Macarena with them. We were all lined up with our hands up, then down on our hips, all the while doing our best pelvic movements. If outsiders had been looking in, they would have been in for quite a sight. Ryan soon stopped and handed me his margarita, and like a true party girl, I went ahead and took a drink. It tasted great, and I nodded in approval at him.

"Brea, this is Krista!" he shouted.

Krista came running right up to me, grabbed me by the arm and pulled me into the house. Ryan followed from behind as he swigged his margarita. He went straight to the kitchen, grabbed another glass and handed me my own. I reluctantly accepted, but grabbed his free arm.

"Hey, I didn't come to party. Can we talk for a second?"

"Oh shit! Really? Come on! Drink up!" he encouraged.

I took another sip to humor him. "Really! I need to speak to you."

"Fuck that! Kiss me first."

"Ryan … I told you I'm with Kale," I said.

"What you can't kiss an old boyfriend now?" he asked all sulky.

"I'll kiss you!" Krista volunteered and jumped onto his front and fervently kissed him right on the lips.

He pulled away and laughed. "Now that's what I'm talking about!"

She jumped down and swished her cute ass into his groin. She had the biggest grin on her sweet, tan face. It occurred to me she was the female version of him. He grabbed her hips and pushed her ass into him. "Yeah, baby!" he shouted.

Without even realizing what was happening, Krista jumped forward and planted a kiss on my lips. I was startled and then frozen. Ryan was roaring with laughter. I looked down at her in shock and gently pushed her away. She pouted her pink-stained luscious lips.

"Honey, I don't swing both ways," I warned. "Ryan!" I shouted, now annoyed. "I need to talk to you!"

"Oh fine! Pooper!" he said and waved me to the other room where he could hear me.

I walked in right behind him. He was still dancing about the room. "Look, I need to know. Why does your dad want me to work for his studio?"

Ryan hardly looked my way. "How the fuck should I know? Dad's an asshole!"

"Come on, Ryan. You must know something," I protested. "You drove up with him. You had to know why."

Ryan took another big swig of margarita just as Krista raced into the room. She pouted and leaned on him. "Come on, Ryan. I want to fuck! Get rid of her. She's boring!"

Ryan looked down and yowled, "Brea? Boring! No way! You got to know her to appreciate her!" He winked at me right as he said the word "know."

Krista seemed unimpressed and began stripping off her little see-through T-shirt to reveal a hot pink, lacy bra. I rolled my eyes. "I'm leaving," I said and turned to go. Just as I reached the front door, Ryan jumped in front of me, swung me around and planted the most passionate kiss on my lips. I had no time to react or do anything to fend him off. He pushed me away, grabbed my hand and thrust it on his junk. I was all at once shocked and slightly turned on, but still determined to get out of there.

"Come on, Ryan! Fuck me," whined Krista from the other room. "I'm ready."

Ryan winked at me one more time. "You'll be back," he said with a grin of assurance.

"Yes, but not to have sex with you," I replied and opened the door and left. I would be back all right. Back to find out why the hell his father was forcing me into servitude!

Chapter 28

I drove home and parked Kale's Mercedes in the apartment complex. I worried it would get broken into while I was inside. My Corolla wasn't half as expensive or as tempting. I walked in through my front door and stopped in my tracks. An unfamiliar guy jumped off Denise with his pants down and his erect dick just waving and saying hello. He immediately tucked himself back in and pulled up his faded jeans. Denise shoved her dress over her hips and looked at me sheepishly.

He extended the hand he had just used to, um, tuck away his manhood and said, "Hi, my name's Jeremiah."

I looked down at his hand, shook my head and started to head for my bedroom. "My name's Brea, and hey, you over there! Lover girl! Your room has a bed. Use it!"

Denise only started chuckling and ignored my comment. "Lance called!"

I didn't respond but walked into my bedroom and shut the door behind me. I pulled my iPhone out of my purse and read a text message from Lance. All it said was he was back in the hospital. "Crap!" I said aloud. I had intended to wait for Kale to come over, so that I could find out what had happened with

Maya. I texted Kale and told him I was going to the hospital just in case he was on his way over. He said he was still in Santa Barbara and to instead meet him later at his house. I agreed and flew out the door to drive to Cedars-Sinai to see Lance.

Once I arrived at the hospital, I checked in at the front desk, but the nurse said Lance was in ICU and couldn't receive visitors. ICU? I was standing at the round desk when I felt a hand come to rest on my shoulder. I turned around. It was the woman I had assumed was Lance's mother. She was short and had salt-and-pepper hair and wore wire-rimmed glasses over her worried eyes.

"Brea?" she asked.

"Yes," I replied.

"I'm Roseanna, Lance's stepmother," she said, which surprised me. "His mother passed. I raised him."

I nodded and shook her hand. "Is he okay?"

"No," she replied with worry written all over her face.

"No?" I said with fear building in the pit of my stomach.

"He got pneumonia again. He lapsed into a coma just hours ago."

"A coma?" I heard myself utter aloud.

A single tear spilled over the side of her right eye and onto her cheek. She looked at me with agonizing pain on her face. I just reached out and hugged her tight. She accepted the gesture even though we did not know each other. I pulled away and looked at her with extreme concern.

"Is he going to die?" I asked.

Roseanna suddenly lost it and dissolved into complete tears. She turned and waved her hand back and forth to tell me she could not speak. I felt terrible for having asked such a question. "I'm sorry, I'm sorry," she repeated twice and looked away.

She moved hurriedly down the hallway and to the restroom where she disappeared inside. I stood there in shock and grief. I staggered toward the parking lot, got in my car and just numbly sat there. I had never lost a friend before. I didn't know how to think or feel. So, I sat in silence, closed my eyes and put my head back against the headrest. I thought about Lance's confession that I was the love of his life. What a love I turned out to be – the girl who could not love him back. The thought of that realization seemed tragic and almost absurd. For some strange, inappropriate reason I started miserably laughing and crying at once. It hit me. I was completely emotionally overwhelmed. My iPhone honked about that time, and I looked down to see a message from Kale that he was home. I decided to drive over and seek refuge in my lover's arms.

Thirty minutes later, I found myself pulling up into the driveway in front of Kale's Spanish-style home. He had left the front door opened, so I walked right in and called out for him. I heard his voice come from the upstairs so I went up. The French doors were wide open and a fire crackled and burned in the fireplace in the far corner. I stopped in the doorway and looked around. Kale was nowhere to be seen. I walked all the way in and turned to find him standing in front of the bathroom in just a white towel. He was sublime to look at, all damp and glistening with water drops still on his chest that he was using another towel to dry off. I took in the sight of his broad, slightly hairy chest and cut muscular arms, Oh! The towel was covering the best sight of all: his ample cock.

"We should probably talk," I said trying to avoid the temptation to rip off that towel.

Kale's eyebrow arched. "Can we talk later?"

"I need to know about Maya," I replied. "What did she say? Why'd she do it?"

Kale sized me up for a moment. "I'll tell you after … "

I sighed and considered the offer. Then I figured why the hell not? Let's have some fun and then confront the nasty reality. Besides, I might not want to have sex if Kale didn't tell me what I wanted to hear. Why waste an opportunity? And truthfully it would give me 30 more minutes to avoid confrontation head-on.

"You don't need that," I said and stepped forward. I smiled and pulled the towel off to reveal his fully naked body. "Ah, there you are," I said in a low, seductive voice.

Kale got the biggest smirk on his face and said, "And you don't need these."

He pulled my pink short-sleeved sweater up and off. He then reached around and easily unlatched my simple white bra and threw it aside. He then lowered himself down to his knees and unbuttoned my black skinny jeans and pulled them down so he was face-to-face with my panties. He smothered his face into my pink-flowered panties, kissing and biting through the thin cotton, which was startling and arousing. Still kneeling before me, he moved his hands around to slowly move up and massage my butt cheeks in each hand. His hands moved in a circular, sexy motion as he continued to use his mouth on the front side. He then artfully used his teeth to pull my underwear down and expose my girlhood. Now that tongue teased and played with me. My head went back, and I sucked in air as lust swirled up through my groin.

"I want to make you cum," he said as he pulled away.

"Oh god!" I cried aloud as his tongue's pace quickened and twirled around my sensitive spot. He then used his fingers in place of himself and pushed and touched with aggression and tenderness. My breath quickened, and I moved my hands to grip his hair, which I wrapped through my fingers so that I could hold on. I thought I might fall over, gripped in such hedonistic delight.

"Oh god!" I cried out again as his tongue moved faster and harder. The wave of pure pleasure built up and built up. Release was soon to come, and then it hit with a powerful, intense force of pure bliss, and quivers and quakes rippled throughout my body. I felt ready to collapse when Kale scooped me up and moved me to the bed. He moved my body vertically on the bed so he could stand, and then he gently moved his hands up my thighs and parted my legs so he could enter me. His huge cock had been hard the whole time, so I knew he was longing to make love, but he had managed to hold back.

He slid into me and worked it slowly to build up his own pleasure. As he stroked me, he used his hands to wander up my stomach to my breasts where he rubbed and massaged them. We hadn't even kissed this whole time, and that's when he leaned and grabbed me by the back of the neck and pulled me up so we formed a V with our bodies. He kissed me hard and passionately. His tongue moved into my mouth and touched my tongue. We played, teased and kissed with such ardor.

He began stroking me hard and harder. I pulled away from his kiss so I could moan and release some of my own tension. Then he managed to pick me up and hold me to him. I began rocking back and forth, using all of my strength to hang on. He now was completely lost in his own crazed delight.

He cried out, "Fuck me harder!"

I obliged and moved as fast as my hips would go. He then bent over and released me onto the bed so he could move at his own pace. He was in a complete lustful frenzy as he went at me. All of a sudden, he cried out louder than I'd heard him do and intensely had an orgasm of seismic enjoyment. His face was red and contorted as he released, and then he fell forward onto me. He was so big compared to me. I felt completely engulfed by his body. He lay on top of me, breathing heavily. I felt his lungs move up and down. He finally managed to move off of me and over to the right side of the bed.

I lay on my back, breathing heavily and staring at the ceiling. Kale turned his head and stared at me. I turned and returned his gaze. He reached out and stroked my cheek. "Sweetheart, you're the best I've ever had," he admitted.

I smiled and nodded. "Takes two," I replied.

He rolled over on his side with his head resting on his

hand. "I love you," he said quietly.

Instead of replying, I leaned into him and kissed him. My head came to rest under his chin, and he rested his jaw on my forehead in a tender way. It was raw and intimate. I loved it. He had made me forget everything that now came rushing back. We needed to talk.

"What are you going to do about Maya?"

"I fired her," he said plainly. "I watched her delete all of the videos, too."

I moved away from him. "She had more than one?" I cried out. "What is her fucking problem? Why would she do such a creepy, sick thing?"

Kale became quiet and thoughtful as he evaluated how to answer that question. "She admitted that she was in love with you. She knew damn well you were straight, but she said if you stayed in my life, she could still be close to you. She liked to watch. Some people are fucking voyeurs, Brea."

"That's — that's just gross! And perverted! What the fuck? And what the hell was she doing stalking me? Fucking hang-ups, dead flowers and live roses? You tell me how I'm supposed to feel about all of this! Everything … and Burt and the studio shit, too!" I yelled in exasperation. "Kale, we need to report her! She's sick!"

"Look, she's also super protective of me. In her mind, the flowers and stalking were meant to help me out. I don't know, Brea; it's fucked up all right. You can't explain fucked-up shit like that. She loves you. She swore she wouldn't hurt you," he defended.

"Kale!" I cried in protest. "We don't know what she'll do. We didn't know she would do this. So, how am I supposed to feel safe?"

Kale now sat up and looked down. "Brea, she won't hurt you. She's going back to Mexico. I've arranged it."

I sat up and threw a pillow at him and got up. "Fuck this shit! Curtis attacks me. You do nothing. Burt wants to procure me. You do nothing but tell me to be a good little girl and go work for the bastard. Now this – and you just pat her on the ass and send her packing? Really? *Really* Kale?"

I went and grabbed my clothes and started to get dressed. Kale moved off the bed and grabbed me by the shoulders. "Sweetheart! It's not like I did nothing; I took care of it. We'll be fine; you'll be fine! Now come back to bed."

"No," I firmly stated. "You're my fiancé, Kale! My protector! Why aren't you protecting me? Is this how it's going to be? I can't trust you to do the right thing."

Kale's eyebrow arched and he glared at me. "You can't trust me? Did you go see Ryan tonight?"

I stared at him. How did he know that? "Yes, but only to find out what he knows."

Kale folded his arms and stared at me. "You should have waited. I would have gone with you. Trust is a two-way street, sweetheart! Can I trust you? What'd you do?"

"What did I do?" I asked incredulously.

"Did you kiss him?" he asked.

"What?" I was shocked. What was going on? Ryan had kissed me, not the other way around. "No," I said flatly.

Kale then went to the night table, grabbed his iPhone and threw it at me. I caught it and looked at the screen. It read: "I kissed your girl, and I liked it." It was from Ryan. I shook my head and replied, *"He* kissed me!"

Kale looked down skeptically. I stood frozen in silence. We were at a complete impasse. I felt tears welling up. I tried not to cry. I stepped forward, and he looked at me. "What does this mean?" I asked.

Kale clapped his mouth tight and shrugged. I shook my head, touched his hand and caressed the top of it. "I'm exhausted. I need to go home."

Kale nodded and wouldn't look at me. I was so lost. I reached forward and wrapped my entire body around his. I felt his muscles loosen, and he managed to hug me fully back. I pulled away, and this time our eyes locked for a moment. I could see his decency, humanity, anxiety, love and caring all rolled up in those blue-green eyes. We stared at each other speechless, and then I turned to leave.

As I reached the threshold of the bedroom, I heard him say softly, "Good-bye, sweetheart."

I turned and looked at him. Then I continued, walked down the stairs, opened the front door and left.

About the Author

Michelle Gamble-Risley is an author, produced screenwriter and CEO of 3L Publishing (www.3LPublishing.com). *California Girl Chronicles: Brea's Big Break* is the second book in the *California Girl Chronicles* series. While running her rapidly growing company, Michelle personally strides to work with new and emerging authors to make their dreams come true to publish their books. She is a passionate lover of books and films and plans to continually work on her own novels and screenplays. You can connect with her on Facebook or follow her on Twitter under MichelleGambleRisley. She loves connecting with fans, so please feel free to email her at Michelle@3LPublishing.com.